I'LL BURY YOU

YOU

TOMORROW

—— ❖ ——

STUART BRAY

For the years forgotten.

CONTENTS

—   ◦   —

HAZEL EYES

Moon City
November 19th, 1999

The dreadful coming of Winter has always had a lasting effect on those of us who have experienced it at its worst, knowing that a time of hardship and stress would soon be upon us. It was November 19th in the year 1999. I sat in my office on the tenth floor of Alan and Brants, a law firm in Moon City that I had been climbing the ladder of for the better part of three years. I considered myself lucky, as I looked down at the swarm of people out on the streets, the everyday people. With a six figure a year income and a penthouse on Bradbury Street, I had it made in every way a man in his thirties could possibly dream of.

"Any plans for the holidays Mr. Birch?" Amy asked, walking through the door I had forgotten to close on my way in. I turned to her with a smile, my hands behind my

back like a big shot. Amy was my assistant, and had been for a little over a month now. She was obviously still getting in the swing of how things operated on the tenth floor.

"No plans for me. I see myself sitting at home in front of a roaring fire with a bottle of wine, watching whichever sports channel I come across first." I smiled, turning back around to look at the flurries of snow racing each other to the sidewalk below. I turned again as I forgot to see what it was that Amy come in for. Hard to forget a body like that.

"Did you need something from me?" I asked, raising my eyebrow and topping it off with a flirtatious grin. Had to show off that expensive cleaning I had yesterday.

"I was actually just coming to ask you if I could maybe have the day before Thanksgiving off. I was going to fly home and see my family. If it seems unrealistic, I'll cancel."

I knew how badly she wanted off; I heard her on the phone at her desk outside of my door talking to someone from back home. She told them that she may be stuck at work and that she would have to ask me if she could have off. I pictured the relative on the other end calling me a tyrant or an asshole. I knew where I would be the day before Thanksgiving. I would be here, buried under a mountain of paperwork with no assistant available to dig me out from the landslide. Amy worked hard and kept a good attitude around the office, maybe she deserved it.

"I realize I haven't been here long enough to be requesting days off like this. You know what? Never mind, I'll call and cancel. I know you'll be here by yourself. I was stupid for asking"

I smiled at her. I was about to be the savior of Amy's holiday, she would squeal and cheer when I said she could have the time off. "Amy, you have proven yourself to be a valuable asset, and you have worked hard for me in the time you've been here. So, of course you can go and see your family for the holidays. I mean, it will be Thanksgiving after all. Next it will be Christmas and you'll need to go home for that as well, I assume." I made sure that she was making eye contact with me so that I could watch all that spunk hit the bricks.

"Go on back to the hick town you crawled out of. Go and see Ma and Pa for biscuits and grits. While you are there stuffing your face, you may want to pop open the county newspaper and look for a job at the local Piggly Wiggly, cause if you haven't caught on by now, if you leave me here to do all of *your* work, then I obviously can't depend on you." That hopeful smile died off just midway through my rant. She looked like such an idiot standing there.

"Now is it family for the holidays, or is it putting in the time at a job you just started?" I asked, turning towards her and crossing my arms. I guess asking her out for dinner tonight was futile.

"I'm- well- I'm sorry Mr. Birch. I'll get back to work. Sorry for bothering you."

She fought back tears as she turned and quickly left my office. It was astonishing that I was made to be the bad guy in this situation. I mean, she just started this job and was already asking for days off. That was the problem with people like Amy, they don't know how to put in the hours. I bet Amy was handed everything in life just because she had a nice body. I knew it for a fact, considering I hired her for that very reason. I could hear her trying to hide her sniffling outside at her desk. She kept clearing her throat over and over.

"Amy, could you please get up and close my door? I am hearing this very aggravating sound and I would like for it to stop." I imagined the look on her face. She sat there, grabbing at tissues, trying to wipe away her running mascara. "You, ok?" I asked as she reached in for the door handle, her eyes all puffy, her makeup smeared like an eight-year-old had applied it.

"Yes, Mr. Birch. I'm fine. Sorry for disturbing you." She nodded at me, then pulled the door closed softly. I tried to fight back the urge to laugh, it was just too hilarious. "Amy!" I called out loud enough that half of the floor must

have turned to see her sobbing like a baby at her desk. The office door opened and there stood crying. Amy, her red dress, her black heals, no stockings on underneath.

"Yes, Mr. Birch?" She asked wiping her face.

"Amy you are so freaking cute, did you think I was serious about not letting you go and see your family? You really think that I'm the kind of monster who would deprive a pretty girl like you the chance for some happiness?" I stood up with my hands on my hips. Amy just stood there as confused as I pictured she would be.

"It's really no problem, Mr. Birch. I can stay and work over the holidays. It was stupid of me to ask with such short notice."

"Nonsense, Amy. You go and see your family for Thanksgiving and Christmas. Hell, go and pay them a visit on valentine's day if you want. I mean, what would someone in my position need an assistant for anyways?" She looked even more confused than before; she stammered not knowing how to respond.

"I'll stay, Mr. Birch. I need the job more. You can count on me."

I smiled at her and shrugged my shoulders. "Well, don't say I didn't give you the chance when the time comes. You're dismissed Amy." I looked down on some random piece of paper on my desk as I waved her away.

I knew that my finding humor in the misfortune of others was odd, I knew it wasn't exactly normal. It's not that I enjoyed it, I just thought it was hilarious that other people took insignificant things in life so seriously. So, Amy would miss one Thanksgiving with her family, maybe next year would be a more appropriate time for her to think about herself. I opened my desk drawer and pulled out a pill bottle with my name printed in small letters across it. I popped two in my mouth and swallowed.

By the time I packed my bag and put on my coat, the office was near empty. Amy still sat with her desk light on, staring at that little green monitor screen, typing away. "I'm heading home, Amy. You finishing up that Fitzgerald report"? I asked knowing very well that she had just started it an hour ago. She looked up at me as if I had just surprised her.

"Yes, Mr. Birch. I'll have it done soon. Hopefully I won't have to walk through the parking garage alone again tonight."

She forced a smile. I knew she wanted to ask me if she could finish tomorrow. If she had, I would have responded with "Maybe if you had spent less time on the phone today, you might have been walking out with me", but she just looked back at her screen and sighed, thinking I didn't hear it. The cab ride back to the penthouse was thankfully pleasant. The driver didn't utter a single word except for some broken English when asking me *"Where to?"*

"Bradberry Street. Penthouse district." I replied, handing him the six dollars and fifty-two cents I would owe at the end of the ride. Guys at the office always asked why I didn't have a nice sports car parked outside. That, or a personal driver pulling up in a new Lincoln. It was simple, I loved my money. I loved my money so much that I didn't spend it on frivolous nonsense, like women and cars. My money went towards making my pad look like my own personal paradise, the perfect getaway from the office and other suits I had to rub shoulders with every day. During the ride, I thought about what tomorrow would be like. Would I get chewed out over the show I put on in front of the office today? I could hear my father giving me the fifth degree already. I reached into my coat and grasped my pill bottle like the feel alone would stop the damn stress.

The elevator took me up to the eighth floor of the ten-story building. I spent my life looking out of a big window, looking down on the street and all of those who couldn't be as big of a success as I was. At times, I felt like God. I looked down on my servants, judging them harshly. The flames in the fireplace cracked like popcorn in the microwave, a fireplace large enough to fit eight large logs at once.

I walked into my bedroom closet, a row of special made Gucci suits on one side, casual clothes on the other. If you were to walk a few feet towards the back of the closet, you would find a shelf covered neatly in the finest handmade loafers and never worn tennis shoes. I remembered specifically requesting that the realtor find me a penthouse with the biggest walk-in closet. After a few failed attempts, the cheap power suit wearing woman finally found one to my liking. I laughed to myself as I remembered assuring her that I would tell my co-workers that were in the market for penthouses and condos to give her a call. I never did. After a nice hot shower in the master bathroom, I slipped on my red and black silk pajamas. I walked past the six-foot mirror that hung on my bedroom wall. Damn, I looked clean.

I opened the two stainless-steel doors on my refrigerator, nothing but half-empty bottles of wine and some two-day-old Chinese takeout. Maybe if I call Amy and threaten her with her job, she'll run me over something from that new Indian place that opened last week. No, I had already walked a fine line today. Luckily, she didn't try and report me to human resources like the last bitch. What was her name? Monica? No, Stacy or something. Stacy or something caught me looking up the short little navy-blue skirt she wore to the office one Friday. She bent over to pick up an eraser cap and before I could advert my gaze, she turned and caught me about to dive in headfirst. The fucking sexual harassment classes I had to attend after the incident were enough to teach me not to stare for more than a second at a time. Stacy or something decided to transfer up a floor or something. The company allowed it. I guess they didn't want the headache of a sexual harassment lawsuit. Man, that chick was a looker, long legs, chocolate brown hair almost down to her perfectly rounded ass. Many nights afterwards, I beat-off just thinking about that black thong being swallowed up those two mounds of genetic perfection.

The phone ringing in the kitchen knocked me out of my fantasy and back into the perfect reality I already lived in. "Who in the hell is calling at this hour?" I asked, storming into the kitchen ready to give someone the ass ripping of a lifetime.

"Hello? Who is this calling at this hour? Are you nuts?" I asked, putting a hand on my hip in grocery store mom like fashion.

"Sorry to disturb you so late, David. Were you busy when I called?"

I didn't recognize the woman's voice on the other end. It wasn't Amy, it wasn't anyone I was familiar with at the office. "Who is this? You better have a damn good reason for calling me, or else the start of your day tomorrow is going to be a shit storm straight out of your worst nightmare." I knew I was being a bit over dramatic, but you had to put your foot down with these kinds of people or they would just continue to try and walk all over you.

"You don't recognize my voice, David? You don't remember me? I guess you wouldn't, now that you sleep so well."

The connection became flooded with static, a loud hissing sound like a deflating tire forced the phone a foot from my ear. "I don't know you, bitch. I don't have time for your games, I'm a busy man. Now, tell me who you are and what it is that you want from me." Through the static I could hear the woman laughing, it made the hairs on my arm stand up straighter than my sexual preferences.

"What a shame, David. You tried to keep me away. It hurts to be forgotten about."

For a moment I could hear the sound of running water, not from a sink or anything, but as if it were filling the room the woman was in. "What the hell is that sound? You by a waterfall? You work at the public pool or something, lady? I never fucked no one like you, trust me. I would have remembered." The woman began laughing even louder, this time it was a maniacal, horrifying laugh. "Are you gargling water or something, lady? What the hell is the matter with you?" I put the phone close up to my ear as the other end went silent, I could hear the woman breathing softly.

"I thought you loved me, David I never thought you would have the nerve to kill me like you did. I was there for you. You treated me like a tumor that needed to be cut out."

I dropped the phone to the kitchen floor. It shattered, the pieces flying in slow motion in different directions. My head started to feel heavy. The room spun so fast that I had to grab the edge of the island counter to hold myself up. That voice on the phone, something about it was so hauntingly familiar. I gagged loudly as I felt my way over to the kitchen sink. I gagged twice more before throwing up the tuna on white I had for lunch. I curled up into a ball underneath my expensive Egyptian cotton sheets. I kept the lamp beside my bed on, the shadows of the room danced around in circles through my sleepless night. I didn't want to think any more about the voice. I wanted to drift off to sleep and erase this night from my memory.

"You need to be better. Try harder, goddamn it. Your mother and I didn't pull all those strings just to have you screw your life up!" My father's voice played over and over like a hit song on the radio. The anxiety made my stomach curl itself into knots.

The sun came through the wall sized window next to my bed. I hadn't closed my eyes once the entire night. I rolled out from under the sheets, I shielded my eyes from the sun that greeted me through the glass. "Goddamn" I sighed, rubbing my temples. My head pounded like someone had dropped a brick on it in the middle of the night. I stumbled to the bathroom like a college freshman after his first party. The motion sensored lights came on as I gave myself a once over in the mirror, dark rings had already begun to form under my eyes. I brushed my teeth and climbed in the shower. The hot water felt so relaxing as it ran down my scalp and onto my face. I needed to be in the office today, I just couldn't show up looking like this. I needed to talk to the doctor about a stronger dose, anything to help with this damn stress. I knew it would get worse and worse the more I thought about it. I shouldn't have pulled that shit yesterday. With my eyes still closed, I reached for the white bar of soap that I kept on a small rack under my shower head. I grasped it tightly in my hand while I scrubbed my face and neck.

"What the fuck?" I asked out loud, feeling a long hair coiled up on the tip of my tongue. I reached my finger in my mouth to scrape the hair off, must have been one from my head. I was the only person allowed to use my soap. Hell, I was the only one allowed in my shower. After spitting out a strangely long black hair, I looked down at the bar of soap. It was covered in long tangled strands of the same hair. "Jesus fucking Christ!" I shouted out in surprise as I threw the soap to the floor of the shower. Snake like strands of black hair were matted up at my feet like some kind of rat's nest. I slammed my shoulder into the glass door as I ran all the way out, back into my bedroom. "What the fuck is going on?!" I asked out loud like someone was in the bathroom who would respond. A puddle of water formed at my feet. An ice-cold chill raced down my spine.

"David, come back in here."

Every muscle in my body locked up like I had just been turned to stone, my heart pounded loudly in my chest.

"David, are you there sweetie? Come get in here with me. I'm getting so lonely."

My jaw wouldn't open. My top and bottom teeth stayed clenched together. I had never felt fear like this before. There was a squeak as the water shut off, I could hear wet feet slapping around on the shower floor. A thud made from a hand pushing open the glass door made my arms tense up tightly to my side.

"You want me to come out there? Have you missed me?" the same gargled voice from last night asked. I wanted so badly to turn around and run. It was like being trapped in a nightmare where you're being chased by a big dog, but you can only run in slow-motion.

"Do you remember when we laid together every night?"

I could see a shadow moving around the corner. It limped and twitched as if it was a VHS tape in fast forward. Instinctively, one of my legs managed to take a step backwards, away from the thing that had me scared shitless. "Who are- who are- you?" I asked through lips as dry as a camel's ass. The figure stopped right before coming out from the bathroom.

"David, you're hurting my feelings"

The woman started to sob, I wanted to run so badly. I knew I couldn't escape this thing. That's when I remembered where it came from.

My eyes shot open. The unknown bikini model stared down at me from the ceiling. Her dripping wet, tan, fit body. The other posters around my room featured sports cars and a beach in Maui. I was late for fucking class again, the second time this week. I threw off the blankets, instantly grabbing any clean article of clothing in arms reach. All the money and connections my father used to get me in here and I was flushing it down the drain with all-night keggers and the occasional line of coke. What class was

I late for? My mind was still trying to see past the haze and confusion of being turned on so quickly. "Professor Gram!" I said out-loud while I pulled on a pair of jeans and a wrinkled polo shirt. I jumped into my Nike's and ran down the steps and out the front door. The house was quiet, everyone else must have made it to their classes on time.

As I tried to sneak into class without being noticed, I was stopped in my tracks by the most wonderful aroma. It was like cotton candy at the fair on a spring night, it made me feel like I was six years old again. Someone must have spent a pretty penny on some damn good perfume.

"Mr. Birch, so lovely for you to join us. We are all so thankful that you decided class was important enough for you to stop by."

I smiled and nodded as I slouched as far down in my seat as possible. Professor Gram was the only Professor in my three semesters of college that actually gave a shit if you attended his lectures or not. He always had to call you out.

"Can any of you tell me about the Burr conspiracy trial of 1807? Are any of your young minds up to the challenge?"

Gram looked around the room, obviously not expecting to see a raised hand in sight. He shook his head unsurprised.

"I'll give it a shot, professor."

A girl's voice called out from the middle row. It sounded fresh and excited, which was odd for this early in the day for anyone attending college. Professor Gram's face lit up as he looked straight ahead at the darkhaired girl in the middle row.

"Awe yes, Miss-

He tried for a few moments to remember her name, which also seemed odd, considering Professor Gram was as sharp as a straight razor and knew pretty much every name of every student who had ever attended one of his classes.

"Stella Novak" The girl responded with an embarrassed giggle.

"Well, Miss. Novak. I'm not sure that I recognize you, but I sure do appreciate your commitment. Please tell me what you can about the Burr conspiracy trial of 1807"

Professor Gram leaned against his desk with his arms crossed, his tacky brown suit and black scarf made him the college professor stereotype. Take all of that and add the fact that his grey hair had completely disappeared from the top of his head only, he had the look down even better than the movies.

"Well, Aaron Burr was the founding father, vice president, and slayer of Alexander Hamilton in their famous duel. He was being tried for treason during the American and French revolution."

The newly discovered Stella went on for about twenty minutes about the trial taking place during an unstable time, both in Europe and in America. I must have spaced out thinking about the stupid shit I had pulled at the party the night before. I'm almost certain that a sophomore named Pam gave me a blowjob in the bathroom. If so, it was kind of hazy.

"Well, I must say that I am impressed with your knowledge of such an important trial that has been sadly buried under the weight of time. I expect your end of semester report to be an interesting read."

Maybe I should stick around for a few seconds instead of being the first one out the door. I needed to get a better look at this chick. For the remainder of class, I stared at the back of her head. I waited impatiently for her to turn around at least to get something from the backpack hanging on her chair. Her long sleeve pink sweatshirt with a white collar sticking out showed that she cared what she looked like, if anything.

"I hope you all enjoy your weekend. Be young and live it up while you still can." Professor Gram called out to the horde of excited students, pushing and shoving their way through the classroom door.

Now was my chance. What do you look like, mystery girl? Stella sat in her chair, still facing the front of the room, almost like she meant to keep me waiting intentionally. She turned her head, just in time to catch my eager eyes waiting. "Wow" I accidently blurted out. I adverted my gaze as quick as I could, what an idiot.

"Something on your mind?" she asked as I began to climb out of my desk. I wasn't a shy person by any means. I had been accused of being a misogynistic, rude, ego maniac who needed to learn when and where certain things were appropriate to blurt out.

"No, nothing on my mind. Just curious about you" I said, trying to play it as cool as I usually did with any chick I felt was worth the time.

"Well, what do you want to know?"

She smiled at me in a way that felt different than all the other girls just looking to party at the frat house. She seemed, almost genuine. "I'd like to know why I've never seen you around before. Someone like you wouldn't have passed by a guy like me without me taking an interest." She was still smiling. She was so goddamn beautiful. Not someone I would loop into the "Hot" group, she was past that. Her eyes were noticeably hazel, even from this distance. Her hair now looked so black that it almost had to be a dye job.

"Well, maybe I just came out of my shell. Maybe I haven't always been noticeable in the eyes of a fraternity president."

She turned away from me after pulling her pink backpack from the back of her chair. My heart dropped and in those few moments. I seemed lost. "Are you doing anything tomorrow night? We are having a party back at the house. You're more than welcome to stop by and chill." My heart raced with hope. I needed her to say yes, I just didn't know why I needed it so badly.

"Is that what you say to all the girls that you invite up to your room? Just come and chill?" she asked without turning back to look at me just yet. I didn't know what in the hell was going on. Something about her very presence made me want to grab her and carry her far away from this place. Even I know I sounded crazy.

"I've had a hundred girls at this school in my bedroom. They've all been forgotten about the second the buzz wears off. I wouldn't want to forget about you." What in the hell was I saying? I didn't know this girl. She didn't know me. I must have sounded like a psycho.

"Wow, David. You are in quite a rush, aren't you?"

She finally turned back to look at me. My body felt warm, my legs trembled, I didn't want to leave this room. This girl was the most beautiful thing I had ever laid eyes on. "Sorry, I don't know what's come over me. I'm not usually like this, I swear." I felt my cheeks heat up like a hot skillet.

"So, you're saying that I get the honor of seeing this whole other side of the guy they call the king of the keg? I have to say, I'm flattered, but I have plans tomorrow night."

The sharp edge of disappointment sliced every limb. The rejection squeezed my throat so tightly that I couldn't catch my breath. "Is it a boyfriend or something? If so, you should blow him off and come anyways." I pleaded, sounding crazier by the second. She looked at me like a sad puppy, her eyes big, her lower lip slightly puckered out.

"Are you asking if I have a boyfriend, David? I suppose I should disclose such information before going any further in conversation with someone who has the reputation that you do." She smirked while raising an eyebrow.

"You've obviously heard a lot of things about me. I can assure you that's not everything that I am. There's this image that I have to uphold. I have to be this person if I ever want to make anything of myself." I couldn't believe the things that were coming out of my mouth. I didn't actually think these things about myself, did I?

"Well David, I believe you. And to answer your question, no, I do not have a boyfriend. Tomorrow night I'm meeting up with some old friends that I haven't seen in ages. But, if you can be patient, I'm free this Sunday"

She flashed a smile that revealed the prettiest teeth I had ever seen. She must have just had them cleaned professionally. Her skin was as pale as fresh milk, her lips and jawline so perfect. She was the most beautiful thing that had ever existed. I shook my head trying to think clearly, I couldn't help myself from going against everything I believed in before catching those hazel eyes. My heart did backflips at the sheer thought of hanging out with this girl. Sunday just felt forever away. "Sunday- yeah. Sunday works, I guess."

She saw right through the act and dissected my expression like a trained FBI agent. *"See, I think the problem is that you have always gotten what you want with those pretty boy looks and daddy never saying no. Maybe you should just take Sunday and be happy about it. It is my choice, take it or leave it."*

Hearing her brutally honest opinion without seeing her face, you would almost think she was being bitchy, but I didn't get that impression. Of course, it sucked ass to have to wait until Sunday to see her again, but what the hell was I supposed to say after all that? "That's a lot to process. No one has ever been honest with me in that way. Sunday works great."

What in the hell was I saying? Any other time I would have called her a tease, a dyke, then tell her to go munch a shag carpet. She smiled and winked as she walked down the steps, then past Gram's desk, then out the door. "Wait!" I called out forgetting to get her number or find out where we should meet up. I leaped, skipping an entire section of steps. I slammed my shoulder into the door. I looked left then right, she was gone. "Shit!" I grunted as I threw my worn-out backpack to the ground. What was I supposed to do? I couldn't run all over campus asking everyone I came across. What would they think of David Birch asking about a chick? They would all assume I had feelings for her, or that I had finally become a one-woman man. The other potentials would think that I was taken and not want to follow me to my bedroom during parties. "Fuck!" I called up at the sky, to the dismay of everyone around me.

"Hey, Davey boy, what the hell are you yelling about? Did an eight out of ten ask for your number?"

I looked to my left to see two other members of Alpha Eta Nu, Tyler Combs and Luke Nelson, staring at me with the same lost to the world stare they always had. They were complete fucking morons.

"You fail a test or something bro? If so, who gives a shit?" Luke said, slapping my back and howling like a big dumb dog.

"I was looking for this chick. I think she's new or something. Didn't get a chance to get her number." I looked around again, hoping I would see her amongst the crowd of chatty students preparing for the weekend.

"You're out here screaming at the sky over some chick? Fuck her. We're going to be rolling in the potential tomorrow night at the party. I need you two dickheads to come to the pharmacy with me on the way. I need to pick up my anxiety meds."

Something angered me about Tyler's comment. It was his lack of respect for this girl he didn't even fucking know, this girl that I couldn't stop thinking about. I gritted my teeth together to keep from flipping out and making a scene. I couldn't have them knowing how I felt right now. It was obvious that they were incapable of understanding. Hell, I didn't understand it myself. "Forget it, let's get back to the house. I'll have one of the pledges make me a steak dinner and chill out." As we walked around like a bunch of ass-slapping monkeys, I couldn't stop hoping that Stella would bump into me around each corner.

By the time we made it back to the house, my mind and body felt so drained, I had never felt so tired in my life. "I think I'm going to head upstairs and lay down. I don't think I'm feeling too hot right now."

"We only walked for like five-minutes bro. How are you tired already?" I heard Tyler call up to me as I fought to climb the cherrywood steps. I wasn't sure why I felt like this. I was in great shape, almost pure physical perfection. Why did I feel so damn tired all of a sudden? I crawled

into bed with my clothes still on. I didn't have the energy to get undressed. I shivered as my teeth chattered loudly. I must have been coming down with the flu, what awful timing it would be if that were the case. One day before the big party. What if I did get to see Stella somehow on Sunday? Would she want to even come within ten feet of me looking the way I did? I drifted off. I had hoped for a peaceful sleep, maybe I would feel better afterwards, the awful nightmares that I experienced felt never ending. I was drowning, every time I tried to scream more and more water was sucked into my lungs, I couldn't wake up.

Walking into my dorm room, I was greeted with my roommate Kelly's ass. "Damn Kelly, why are you always naked?" I asked trying to look serious and hold back the urge to bust out in laughter. Kelly turned to look at me like a deer in headlights.

"Oh, shit, Stella. I didn't think you were coming back to the room. Thought you were meeting up with your friends early."

She covered herself with her polka dotted comforter, her tattoo covered body still visible. "I needed to come and get my bag with the clothes and stuff I packed. I have to get out of these clothes. Looks like you needed to do the same." I finally started laughing as I closed the door behind me. Kelly had been my roommate during my entire time at N.K.U. We were opposites that attracted right away. "Let me ask you something, Kelly. Do you know a guy named David Birch? He's a frat guy over at the frat house that throws all those parties." Kelly thought for a moment before her eyes grew and her mouth dropped open.

"Oh yeah, I know him. My friend Courtney slept with him I think. Why are you asking about a douche like that?"

Kelly was now fully dressed. She had on some metal band that I had never heard of, wasn't really my type of music. We've had matching black hair ever since she talked me into dying it. Kelly wasn't a bad influence, just not the best.

"He started talking to me in Grams class, acted like he was seeing me for the first time and invited me to *'chill'* at the frat house tomorrow night."

Kelly smiled at me. I knew she was about to make a joke out of it. *"Are you going to 'chill' with a frat guy, Stella? Is he going to be like a one-night boyfriend or something?"* She laughed hysterically as she sat down at her vanity and started applying black lipstick. Kelly had tried her hardest to get me to drop the basic look and come to *'the dark side'*. I just loved my clothes and makeup too much to change now. She popped open the little yellow pill bottle that she kept in her drawer, she said they were for stress.

"He has the reputation of a man whore who sleeps with every girl he meets. I'm not sure I want to be one of those girls."

I shrugged.

Kelly turned around smiling, here she goes again. *"You haven't slept with a single guy since I've known you. Aren't you a little curious to jump in his bed and see what all the fuss is about? I mean, personally, I think you should avoid that guy and his house like the plague. I knew a guy who at that frat house, turned out to be an asshole."*

I shrugged. "The funny thing is, he seemed genuine. I feel like he opened up to me in the few minutes that we spoke. I mean, I didn't help matters when I was being flirty. Hell, I even left him hanging without giving him my number or dorm room." Kelly and I laughed *together* this time. From the corner of my eye, I could see the empty twenty-gallon tank still filled with wood shavings and a small food bowl. "Poor Rufus" I thought only to myself, not trying to open any wounds that hadn't yet healed.

"Damn, girl. If he really does want you, he must be going crazy not having you being a guaranteed thing. And by the way, he is a master of what he does. Don't trust that 'opening up' thing. A guy like that knows what to say to get into your pants. Best thing you can do is just make him fight for it, or just say screw him all together."

I knew Kelly was right, when it came to this subject there was no use in trying to argue with her. She may have not been the best influence style wise, but she never steered me wrong.

"So, do you think the spell worked?" I asked before a moment of silence covered the room like a sheet of ice. Kelly looked over at me using the mirror of vanity. She glared at me like I had just told her '*black*' wasn't actually a color.

"It was a stupid Joke. I'm not a witch, and none of my spells have ever worked on myself. Trust me, it would've helped in high school. It's probably that new hair color, or the fact that you started wearing that push-up bra that you don't actually need."

I felt the need to break the tension with a half-smile. A few weeks ago, Kelly and I were having a small pity party by ourselves in the room. Kelly brought a big bottle of rum that tasted like rubbing alcohol and coconut. While we were taking massive swigs from the now half-empty bottle,

Kelly blurted out in a drunken stupor that she dabbled in witchcraft when she was a kid.

"Just typical white girl basic ass magic, ya know? I was like casting spells on all the little bitches in my grade. Shit never worked but once."

Her head bobbled for a few seconds as she looked around the room. I could tell she was fighting to not barf all over our new pink faux bearskin rug. The mixture of her pills and alcohol couldn't sit in her stomach too much longer. I laughed as she started giggling, trying to hand the bottle to me but couldn't lift it more than a few inches off her lap. I think we were both feeling a lot better after being left off of the guest list for Delta Khi's party. "Fuck those bitches, they don't know dick!" I joked as I hoisted the bottle up high in the air, almost hitting the ceiling fan.

"Girl, you are too pretty not to be noticed. You should be running this place. Every bitch-ass sorority should want you to pledge. But naw, you're bunking in the dorms with my fat ass... again. Its bull."

I laughed as she almost tipped over on her side, the bottle wrapped in her arms like it was a small child that she needed to protect at all costs. "I've never been noticed like that. I mean, I know I'm not ugly. Not to sound conceited or anything." I laughed, knowing that there was no chance at not sounding stuck up with a comment like that. "I've always had to initiate everything. Guys just walk right past me until I drop a book or clear my throat loud enough for them to glance over." Kelly was either puckering out her bottom lip because of my sob life story, or her face was starting to melt.

"You deserve so much more. No chance you're looking for a female companion?" Kelly asked, holding back the urge to cry with laughter. Her cheeks grew round and full of air, her eyes bulged, and her oversized busty chest bounced with anticipation to cackle like a hyena.

"I really like you and all Kelly, but I don't think I'm ready to move our beds together just yet." I smiled as I grabbed the bottle from her grasp. She couldn't hold it any longer. Kelly fell to her side like a Weeble wobble, she rolled in laughter.

"I'd break your skinny ass!"

She amused herself far too often. Imagining her laughing at a comment made by someone else was almost impossible. She always had to add pepper to an already seasoned dish. "You want to do some magic that makes me irresistible?" I asked, tilting the bottle back and letting the last swig of rum to trickle down my throat. I looked at the empty bottle and then back at Kelly. For a moment, I was startled that someone as intoxicated and goofy as Kelly could change their demeaner at the drop of a hat. She sat so still that it was almost like she was frozen in time, her eyes not leaving mine to even blink.

"If you ask me to, I'll do it. I'll do it if that's what you really want. This shit never works for me. I bet it would work for a person as good hearted and pure as you."

Her voice almost sounding robotic, like she was programed to say such as thing the second I brought up her past in black magic. A chill crawled down my spine like a giant centipede chasing a hairless baby mouse.

"I've known you long enough to tell, you're a good person who hasn't done shit to hurt anyone. I fucking feel it. But, if you had done something terrible before now, this shit could backfire and come after anyone around you."

I couldn't tell if it was the alcohol and pills doing the talking for Kelly, or if she just suddenly snapped out of her drunken stupor. She seemed almost like a different person entirely. "I mean, I don't know. What exactly would we have to do?" I asked, trying to be serious. It was a difficult room to read. Kelly certainly seemed genuine. She didn't answer, she looked around the room for a moment before landing on the tank that her pet rat Rufus sat in, looking out at us curiously. "Is Rufus a magic rat? Is he going to turn me into a princess if I kiss his fury little ass?" I asked falling back to stare up at the ceiling. It was a big secret that

Kelly even had Rufus in the first place. The dorms didn't allow pets of any size, especially a fat brown rat.

"Rufus plays a major role in the spell. He will be a living sacrifice."

The word *'sacrifice'* took a moment to register in my brain. When it finally did, I sat up in shock. "A what? You're kidding, right?" I watched as Kelly scooped Rufus from his cage, just as he had shoved a large green treat into his little cheeks. "You're not serious, Kelly. Put Rufus back, you're going to scare the daylights out of the poor thing." I had grown fond of Rufus in the time living in the dorms with Kelly. At first, not so much, but after a few weeks of waking up and seeing him staring at me through those big brown eyes while chewing on his food like a squirrel in the front yard, I had grown to love him, in a weird sort of way.

"Pull the rug out from under my bed. We'll need that and some of your red lipstick. Oh, and grab those black candles from the top of the closet."

It seemed that somehow Kelly's buzz had worn off and she was now in nut job mode, I watched her carry Rufus over to her vanity. She grabbed a pair of large scissors from the drawer. "Kelly, what in the hell are you going to do? This is insane, let's just forget about it and watch the craft. You love that movie, remember?" I tried to plead with her, but she acted as if I were a hundred miles away. To be honest, it freaked me out enough that I did as she asked without another word. After I finished pulling the soft black rug from under Kelly's bed, grabbing the candles, and a tube of my most expensive lipstick. I had everything ready for whatever this was.

"We almost ready?" Kelly asked as she pulled the metal chain on the light. The room went dark, only the flickering flames of the candles lit up our shadowy faces. Kelly popped open my lipstick, she drew a large five-pointed star on the black rug in front of her. I looked up at her, still hoping this was all some kind of joke. She then drew a circle around the star, making a big red pentagram. I wasn't a religious person per se, but looking down at that star gave me chills. A sickly feeling ran up my stomach. It just sat there, waiting.

"I am so sorry, Rufus. You had meaning in life, and so do you in death."

I watched in complete horror as Kelly closed the blades of the scissors around the fat neck of her beloved Rufus. He squeaked loudly before his head landed with a thud in the center of the pentagram. "Jesus fucking Christ, Kelly! What in the hell is the matter with you?" I asked as I jumped to my feet to avoid the spritz of rat blood. "Are you just drunk, or out of your fucking mind?" I asked still backing up from the horrific scene of animal carnage.

"I had to do it, Stella. It had to be done. You have to have a sacrifice before the ritual."

I expected Kelly to be at least a bit sad about chopping of the head of our dorm pet. She only seemed wide eyed and crazy, almost like a feral cat living behind a dumpster. "You mean that wasn't the ritual? You just cut off Rufus' head. That was just the start?" I asked, mortified and slightly confused. I sat back down after an almost three-minute stare down from Kelly, still holding the twitching body of Rufus. "Let's get this over with. I'm not drinking rat blood by the way, don't even think that shit is going to happen." I said pointing a finger as I sat Indian style across from Kelly.

"What happens next will require you to be completely still. If you move even an inch, this was all for nothing. Do you understand?"

Without saying a word, I just nodded. I mean, what could be worse than what I had just witnessed my room- mate do to a helpless animal?

"Close your eyes, Stella."

I did as I was told.

"Eyes of hazel sitting in the dark, take this offering as we do our part. Turn this blood of innocent life, take this soul and do as you like. As good in spirit as she is at heart, give

this girl a brand-new start. Make her the desire of the men who seek, their strength gone, and their minds grow weak."

As I listened to Kelly, I made sure to keep my eyes closed. I would play along with her momentary lapse of sanity, and then, in the morning, I could scold her for being a complete psycho when she drinks rum. As the room grew quiet, I could feel a warm liquid running down my scalp and on to my face. I wanted to run and scream, but I knew I couldn't. If Kelly would go through these lengths to prove that she was some kind of Witch, what would she do if I messed this up?

My alarm going off startled me so badly that I rolled out of bed and onto the floor below. "What in the hell? What kind of messed up dream." I pulled the covers off of my head to look around the room. No pentagrams, no blood, no Kelly. "Rufus?" I asked crawling over to the table that his tank sat on. "Are you still alive?" The tank was empty, just a food bowl and some wood shavings. "What the hell?" I asked looking down at my blood covered shirt. I jumped to my feet and ran over to Kelly's vanity mirror. I screamed at the sight of the dried blood that coved my hair and face.

"David!? Bro, are you awake or not? You've been asleep forever. We have party in like four hours."

The sound of one of the brothers cawing at my door awoke me from my third or fourth fever dream. I looked around the dimly lit room, I wondered what time it was and how long I had been out. I rubbed my head, it ached from dehydration. My stomach growled like a cornered hound. "The party is Saturday, leave me the hell alone." I huffed as I buried my face back in my sweat covered pillow.

"It is Saturday, dumbass. You've been asleep since you came home yesterday. I'm not going to be your mommy and wipe your ass. The brothers need the president front and center before this party."

I looked around the room confused, the same way you would feel taking a nap after school as a kid. You wake up after a few hours thinking it's the next morning. I rubbed my eyes. I felt a lot better than I had when I had slipped into this sudden comatose state. "Let me get dressed and take a shower. I'll be down in a few minutes." I heard footsteps depart from the front of my sealed fortress of solitude, a frustrated mumbling followed. I got out of bed.

I could feel the dried sweat that had encased me like another layer of thick skin. My mouth had become so dry from my lack of hydration that I could feel the flakes of dried skin peel from my lips. As soon as I cleared my mind and set a clear objective, the first thing I saw, as if it were pasted on the front of my forehead, was Stella. "Shit, when were we supposed to hangout? Was she supposed to be coming to the party tonight? No, she's hanging out with friends tonight. Tomorrow night is the night we decided on."

I hadn't even realized that I was talking out loud to myself. "Besides, I don't even know where she lives. Does she live in a sorority? Adorm? Shit, I have no idea." I paced around the room looking for a towel and a change of clothes for after my way overdue shower. The hot water hitting my skin was enough to wake me the hell up. I could feel the dried sweat turn into a thin slime that puddle at my feet at the shower floor. I closed my eyes tightly as I scrubbed my hair rigorously with my nails, the shampoo ran down my face and through the little bit of facial scuff that I could grow.

"David"

I jumped clear out of my body and did a lap around the earth before returning to my body at the sound of a woman's voice on the other side of the shower curtain.

"Jesus Christ, I'm in the shower!" I said, trying to catch my breath through the thick steam. "My door was locked for a reason. How the hell did you get in here?" I didn't know if I should be freaked the hell out or angry.

"David, you did this to me. Why did you do this?"

I wiped my face in the stream of hot water as quickly as I could. It took a moment for my eyes to adjust to the figure standing on the other side of the fogged over plastic curtain. "Who in the hell are you, Bitch? How did you get in here? Did Tyler let you in? The party doesn't start for a few hours. Get in line outside my door if you want time in here." The figure just stood there, not moving. I wanted to rip open the curtain so badly. My hands just stayed rested on my face, the gut-wrenching fear that I now felt didn't allow to move.

"I had so much planned. So much life still to live."

The figured reached up and put a hand over the shower curtain rod. It was pruned and discolored, the fingernails chipped and caked with pieces of hair and blood. I swallowed hard and closed my eyes, and in one swift motion, I lunged forward towards the figure. The pops of the rings ripping from the curtain rod where all I could hear as I crashed onto the floor, wrapped in the wet plastic. I jumped up as quickly as I could to confront the figure, only there was no one there. "Where are you!?" I shouted at the top of my lungs.

"What in the hell are you doing in there, David? It sounded like you were about to come through the goddamn floor."

I ignored Tyler as he yanked loudly on my door handle. I looked behind the bathroom door, under my bed, and in my closet... Nothing.

"Are you okay or not bro? We are all waiting for you."

"I'm getting dressed, Tyler. Give me a freaking second to breathe, damn!" I growled in frustration. For good measure, I checked my bedroom window. It was still locked from the inside. "What was that?" I asked myself, still hearing the women's voice. As I walked down the steps, dawning the douche attire that I had chosen without much thought. "I'm here. Everyone can calm down and quit crying like little babies needing mommy's tit." I mumbled, not even caring to look my frat brothers in the eyes as I nudged past them to get to the front of the living room.

"What's up his ass?"

I heard a voice whisper before everyone in the room started to snicker like middle schoolers after hearing someone fart in class. I turned around the second I reached the front. My eyes darted around the room, looking for the first person with even the hint of a grin on their face. "I've been sick. If any of you actually gave a shit, you would know that." I snapped at a now church quiet crowd of gelled hair and frosted tips. "Did any of you care to come check on the president? Did anyone get a pledge to make me soup or wipe my ass?" I looked around as all fifteen of my *'brothers'* lowered their heads with guilt. "Now, let's talk about this party tonight." A roar of applause erupted.

"I think I might show up at that party tonight?" I said with a shrug as I popped open a bag of potato chips from the hallway vending machine. I looked over at Kelly to see if she had heard me, not surprising, she was staring down the hall like a zombie. "Kelly, did you hear me?"

A startled Kelly looked over at me like I had just shouted in her ear. *"What is it?"* She asked like I had just shaken her out of a deep sleep.

"I said I might go to that party tonight at David's. Maybe catch him in the act being the lady legend that everyone claims that he is." I laughed as I popped a grease covered chip into my mouth. Kelly looked back down the hall and then back at me, her eyes like frisbees.

"Are you seeing that?"

She pointed down the hall. I noticed her face was more ghost white than usual. I looked in the direction that Kelly pointed, her long black painted fingernail aimed directly down to the closed double doors where a few other students were hanging out, laughing at jokes I was too far away to hear. "I see some people laughing, I see two red double doors, and that's about the extent of it. What is it I should be seeing right now?" I asked curiously. Kelly looked back over at me, her face even paler than before, her eyes uncomfortably wide. I heard her whisper something unintelligible before turning and running down the hallway in the opposite direction. "Kelly! What is it? I don't see anything."

I turned again to see if I had missed something, I saw nothing out of the ordinary. As I entered our dorm room a few minutes later, I noticed that the lights were still off from when we left earlier. "Kelly, you in here?" I asked flicking on the switch.

"Turn off the light!" Kelly's voiced cried out from an unknown location in the room. I did as she asked.

"I messed up, Stella. I messed up so bad. There is something coming for me, all because I did that spell. You're a good person, it shouldn't be like this."

I could hear the razor-sharp fear, deep in Kelly's voice. "Kelly, I don't understand what is going on. What is it you think you saw in the hallway?"

I could now hear her heavy breathing as I shut the door closed behind me. "Where are you? Let me help." I pleaded in the darkness. I was just about to say screw it and turn back on the light when out of the corner of my eye, I saw movement. I stood there for a few moments, my heart racing in my chest, knowing I was about to be frightened. "Kelly, just say where you are. It's too dark in here and I'm not about to be surprised when you pop out." I tried to play it cool, but in my very soul, I knew something was terribly wrong here.

"How do I know if it's the real you? How do I know that you're not the one I saw in the hall? She looks just like you."

A chill that felt like a bucket of ice-water being poured over my head ran through me like a bolt of lightning. "What are you talking about, Kelly? It's me, the only me."

I could hear her breathing grow louder and louder. It sounded like it was coming from under her bed. I felt my way through the room, I could feel the headboard of Kelly's bed. I kicked an empty pill bottle with my right foot, it rolled across the floor before stopping at one of my dirty shirts. "Are you under here?" I asked hoping deep down that she wasn't. "Kelly?" I slowly got down on my knees, I leaned down even slower.

"Get the fuck out!"

I jumped back, hitting the back of my head on something in the dark. Kelly had crawled out of the darkness beneath the bed, only to scream in my face. My heart was beating so fast that I couldn't breathe. "Kell- Kelly, what the hell?" I asked, rubbing the lump on the back of my head. Kelly crawled out from under her bed like something form a Japanese horror movie. I had never been so freaked out in my life.

"That spell. It wasn't right. I wasn't right."

Kelly dropped to the floor in front of me. She sobbed loudly as she began violently shaking my shoulders. "Kelly, stop. What are you talking about? That was just all bullshit that got a little weird from the alcohol. You're scaring the hell out of me right now."

Kelly wrapped her arms around me as she cried even harder. Was she on something? She seemed so spaced out earlier. "Did you decide to do some partying without me?" I laughed as I leaned back, trying to get a glimpse of her tear drenched face.

"What did you do that you didn't tell me about, Stella? Did you do something in the past? Something that would make you not a deserving person?"

Kelly put her cold hand on my cheeks. My eyes started adjusting to her face, her black makeup smeared all over it. "What do you mean? Have I ever done something bad?" I was confused by the question, what did my past behavior have to do with Kelly's freakout?

"A spell that makes you desirable only works right on someone honest and pure at heart. I've never heard you mention anything you've ever done wrong. I assumed you were just an all-around good person."

I wondered if Kelly could see the look on my face. If she could, she may have gotten offended. "I am a good person. Kelly, I may have done some things in high school that weren't so great, but that was a long time ago."

I thought back to high school. On the rare occasions that I did, only one name came to mind. Scott Graft. Scott was my boyfriend sophomore year at Glenville High. It was the first relationship either one of us had up to that point. Scott and I were both loners. Neither of us ever really had the cliche group of friends that you saw in the movies, just two quiet kids with a lot in common. So, after a few conversations about Shakespeare and cheesy movies, we were officially a *'thing'*. After a few months, I started to notice little things about Scott that got under my skin, things that just plain annoyed the hell out of me.

"I didn't hear from you last night. Was everything ok? I don't understand why you couldn't just answer the phone and let me know that you were thinking of me."

He would go on and on the next day if we didn't talk on the phone that night. I would be accused of being with another guy, not caring about his feelings, growing tired of him; it never ended. That was, until my seventeenth birthday party.

My birthday took place on one of the hottest days of the summer. I mean like, record book hot. So, my mom suggested I have some friends over for a pool party.

"Just a few friends. We'll cook some hamburgers on the grill." I remembered her saying over my excitement.

I was on the phone almost instantly. I called a few of friends I had gained over the years of living in the same neighborhood, only most of them went to private schools that were a bit too *'uppity'* for my parents' tastes. After calling the measly five friends that I could think of, I started to dial Scotts number. I stopped and thought for a moment about how clingy and touchy he could be when I was around other people. If I didn't invite him, how would he ever know? None of the people coming to the party even went to our school. This would be a fun and enjoyable night away from all that neediness. Well, long story short, Scott pulled up to my house after the party had been going on for a few hours. He must have heard the music and splashing out on the back deck.

"What the hell, Stella? Are you having a birthday party? I've been calling you non-stop and your mom just keeps saying that you're hanging out with friends."

I looked around at my neighborhood friends. They all sat quietly on their floats, waiting to see how I was going to respond. I felt the embarrassment burn my cheeks, but it was nothing compared to how fed up I was. "You didn't get invited, Scott, because I needed a minute without you up my ass. You are so clingy that I can't stand having you around every waking second. This is my party, and I can invite whoever I want. If you don't like it, get over it." My friends laughed as Scott started kicking the deck box next to the pool.

"I loved you, Stella. I put my life into this relationship. How could you do this to me and not feel a thing?"

I shrugged my shoulders and laughed along with my guests. Scott kicked the deck box again, just as my mom and dad walked out on the back deck.

"If you're going to disrespect our property, you should leave and not come back." My dad said sternly as he placed a plate of buns out on the table. I looked over at Scott, his face now flushed, his knuckles now ghostly white from squeezing his fists so tightly. At this moment, I felt bad

for what I had done. He must be so embarrassed. How could I treat him like that? Before I could say a word, Scott had turned around and ran up to his little white truck and peeled off down the road.

"What a psycho." Someone called out behind me before cannonballing into the pool.

I laid in bed that night staring up at the ceiling. I couldn't help but think about what Scott had been through tonight. But I was young, he was young, we had our whole lives ahead of us and would move on from each other before we were even out of high school. There was so much I wanted to do before I had to go to college and work. I wanted to enjoy being young. The next day my mom got a call from Scott's mom, telling her that Scott had flipped his truck into an embankment coming home from my house. He was dead before he made it to the hospital. At first, I remember being overwhelmed with grief. I couldn't eat, I couldn't sleep. Once I made it to my senior year, Scott was a distant memory, a time forgotten.

I looked up at Kelly, still sitting in the darkness.

"Something terrible is going to happen to you Stella, and there's nothing I can do to stop it."

"Goddamn, Kelly. I'm over this shit. That little spell you did was nothing. The most serious thing that came out of that night was you cutting off your pet rat's head. That was seriously messed up, and I think you feel so guilty about it and you're so ashamed and embarrassed that you start making up crazy stories."

I took a deep breath after my tirade. "I am going to a real party tonight, not some animal sacrifice nut fest sitting here with you." I stood up and walked towards the light from the hall that shown under the door. "Have fun with whatever it is you're doing." I slammed the door behind me. I was held back enough in high school; I am not being held back here. I was livid as I marched down the hall and down the stairs. "How dare her. How dare her go and get wasted on whatever it was she was wasted on, and then come and pull that crazy crap on me." I mumbled to myself as I stomped like a child down the concrete steps. I was going to that party; I was going to take advantage of whatever the reason I was noticed the way I was today.

"Let the festivities begin!"

Bret called out at the top of his lungs before crashing onto the floor, the foam from his beer flying across the room and hitting some random chick in the head.

"Someone get him upstairs." I snapped my fingers as two pledges (I couldn't remember the names of) scurried in like little servants to scoop Bret's unconscious body up from the floor. "Put him in his own bed, not mine. Stay the hell out of my room!" I commanded the pledges as they struggled to get Bret's dead weight up the winding staircase. I shook my head and put myself back on the clock, I had to find that lucky girl that would inevitability follow me up to my room. I scanned the room like the terminator, trying to lock on to a potential target. "Stella?" I asked before my jaw dropped to the floor.

"Hey. Surprised to see me, Mr. president?" She asked as she approached with a smile that must have been practiced in front of a mirror over the span of a decade.

"I'm very surprised. I thought you had something with friends or something tonight. I didn't get a chance to get your number or where you were staying." She laughed at whatever I had just asked, or said, my brain couldn't process which I had just done. Stay in the game you moron. She's just some beautiful chick that you won't even remember after she leaves your bed in the morning.

"Something came up, so I decided to stop by and see what all the fuss was about."

The most beautiful girl I had ever seen in my life just happened to stop by. She just happened to have no plans tonight. "I doubt someone as beautiful as you had nothing going on tonight. There's no way. What sorority are you in? I've never seen you at any parties." I asked over the loud music playing in the background.

"I live with a roommate in the dorms, I never pledged a sorority, and I really had nothing going on tonight."

She laughed as she moved closer, probably so she could hear me better. "Do you want to go upstairs so we can talk? I can't hear a thing down here." I knew how that sounded, but for once, it wasn't some kind of line to get a girl upstairs. I genuinely wanted to hear what she had to say. She rolled her eyes at me with a cute half smile.

"Yeah, I'm sure all you want to do is sit on your bed and talk." She responded sarcastically.

"Wait no, I'm serious. I really want to know more about you. It's not like that." I hoped the seriousness behind my eyes and the way that I touched her arm, assured her that I had no ill intentions. She raised a suspicious eyebrow, then gestured for me to lead the way. Just being around her made me forget all about the craziness from earlier, this girl was special. As we ascended the staircase, we received countless side stares and heard multiple whispers that we couldn't make out over the fading music.

"This is me." I gestured towards the door with the handwritten *'off limits'* sign, scotch taped neatly for any wandering party goers. "I usually keep it pretty clean. Today, not so much. Too much on my plate with planning the party." I was kind of embarrassed for Stella to see my bedroom in the state it was currently in, definitely not a place I wanted a girl like her to have to see.

"My roommate and I are pretty bad about picking up after ourselves. Trust me, it can't be any worse."

Her words sounded so reassuring. Never did I care about what a girl thought about my bedroom. I opened the door and braced myself for the look on her face. Surprisingly, she just shrugged like it wasn't so bad after all. "I have an extra chair over here at my desk, if you feel more comfortable sitting in it than the bed." I scurried over to grab the office chair from my desk, this was also a first for me. I had more girls on my bed this semester then I could count on both hands. I didn't want Stella to be like them.

"I'm fine sitting on the bed, if you don't mind it."

After she smiled, I felt a fluttering feeling deep in my stomach. I think it was what people called *'butterflies'*. I had never had that feeling over any random. "I don't mind at all, just didn't want to come off like that's where I was trying to get you."

I laughed awkwardly as I sat down next to her. She was wearing a short navy-blue sundress with little yellow flowers on it. My heart raced as her boobs slightly bounced when she sat down on the bed. What in the hell was wrong with me? I had to snap out of this shit. I wasn't the falling in love type. I didn't ever want to be tied down to one person. I freaked out and stood up. "Look, I don't know how or why I'm feeling the way I do about you. I barley know you. It feels like some weird shit is going on. I was sick as hell with a fever that knocked me out for the better part of a day, I saw some creepy shit when I was in the shower, and I feel this strong connection to you. We've only talked for the first time yesterday." I looked down at Stella still sitting on my bed. She looked shocked, scared, and perplexed all at once.

"I'm sorry for unloading that all on you. I don't know why I did that, it was rude." Now I was apologizing to some chick? Now it was undeniable that something was wrong with me. I remember my dad always saying, *"Never say sorry to a woman. You start saying sorry, she owns you."* Looking back on my dad's advice, I realized he sounded a bit like an overzealous prick. Stella took a deep breath, then stood up.

"This is going to sound really stupid, so please don't judge me too harshly."

Here it comes. I ruined my chance with Stella, she is about to tell me I sound like some paranoid, obsessive nut case. She walked over to a picture of my mom and dad I had sitting on a bookshelf, she picked it up for a moment before sitting it back down.

"My roommate has dabbled in black magic since she was younger. The other night she did some kind of spell on me that would make me irresistible to the first-person that I drew attention to. I know it was all bullshit and I know that isn't what's happening to you. I'm just saying that- honestly, I don't know what I'm saying or why I'm saying all this to you. I guess watching my roommate go through whatever it is she's going through has made me realize how much stress is put on us as young adults."

I stood up, raising my hands to cut her off. "A spell? You had your roommate do some spell to get my attention? That sounds- I don't want to be rude, but that sounds a little fucking crazy." I bit my tongue before I could say anything else that made me sound like an insensitive asshole. I tried to read her emotions, it seemed that she was expecting that reaction.

"I'm not saying I agree with it or even believe it. I'm just saying that we all feel pressured in a place like this, and the

weight of the stress can make us believe crazy things. I mean we have mid-terms coming up and we are all feeling the effects that come with that."

I shook my head. I knew there was a catch here. "Are you saying that I came down with a random one-day fever, then saw some creepy chick standing in my bathroom, obsessing over you, all because I'm stressed about mid-terms? I don't know what sounds crazier, your roommate being a witch or that you feel you know me enough to diagnose me. I will be honest, I am stressed as shit. I have to pass this mid-term, I have to leave collage and get on the road to becoming a lawyer." I glanced over at my dad's stern face in the photo on my shelf. If I wasn't stressed before, I sure was now that someone who had gotten inside my head told me that I was. "So, I'm not under some spell, I'm just stressed out? Is that your diagnosis, doctor? I thought this was law school." I rolled my eyes. This night wasn't going the way I had planned.

"Stress comes in different ways for all of us. My roommate believes she is some closeted witch, I think I'm all of a sudden beautiful, and you think you're in love with a random girl."

I turned back at her. I couldn't believe what a conceited bitch she had turned out to be. "I never said anything about love. I- I- what the hell is this, anyways? Are you really blaming all of this on stress? You have no idea what stress is. No idea what it's like to have a father who pushes and pushes you until your soul breaks into a million pieces. Don't act like you know me." I could feel the vein in my forehead throbbing, my body heat came through my polo collar in the form of hot steam.

"You pushed me away. I could have been something, you forgot me."

"What?" I turned back to an even more confused Stella.

"What? I haven't had a moment to respond to your tirade."

"You didn't just say something about pushing you away? It sounded like your voice." I looked around the room, the thought of the girl from the shower came crashing into my mind like a semi-truck.

"I haven't said anything. I was going to tell you to chill out, but obviously you need more than that."

Stella stood up and sighed loudly. This night was a complete wreck. One minute, this girl was all I could think about, I wanted nothing more than to make her happy. Now, I just wanted her to get the hell out of my room so I could continue on with the rest of my night. "I guess you're leaving. Sorry I wasn't the guy you thought I was." She turned to me, oblivious to sarcasm.

"Honestly, you are exactly the guy I thought you would be. I should have listened to Kelly and not come here at all."

I stood up next to her fast enough that she jumped slightly back in surprise. "Your roommate's name is Kelly, like as in Kelly Frost?" I asked, completely dumfounded. I knew now what was going on here, this was all some kind of game to get back at me. That freaky dyke Kelly was out to get me.

"How do you know Kelly? She doesn't come to these date rape parties, and I know she doesn't have any classes with you."

I shook my head and laughed. I should have known this was too good to be true. "That freak came to our Halloween party last year, tried to hook up with my buddy Tyler. He kicked the crazy bitch to the curb once she took her shirt off. I'm guessing you know why." I watched her process the information I had just dropped like a bag of bricks.

"She said she went out with friends on Halloween. She never said she was coming to a party, especially a party here. And I'm guessing your douche-bag buddy didn't like Kelly's tattoos. I guess she wasn't the preppy little whore that usually comes to these things."

I was growing tired of the insults. This bitch had already insulted my fraternity, my friends, and myself. "How did you get my attention the way you did in class? At least tell me that. Why couldn't I stop thinking about you? It's obvious that it wasn't your '*charming personality*', so what was it? Better yet, how the hell did you get in my room when I was in the shower?" Her expression changed in the blink of an eye.

"*What in the hell are you talking about? I was never in your room, and the only reason you noticed me was because I died my hair and pushed my tits up. Is it that hard to understand how your caveman brain is wired?*"

She turned to walk towards the door but bumped her leg against the desk chair that had my jacket draped over it, my pill bottle hit the ground like a dropped maraca. Stella looked down at the little orange see through bottle.

"*Diazepam?*" She asked looking back up at me.

"Yeah. What's it to you? Collage is fucking stressful. Ninety percent of the kids at this school are on some type of anxiety medication. Are you going to say that you're not? You sounded like a damn plastic easter egg full of rocks coming up the steps. I could hear the rattling even over the music." I watched her slowly reach into her pocket to feel for something before pulling out her hand.

"*I don't have to explain shit to you. I'm leaving.*"

"You're not going anywhere until you tell me how you got in my bathroom earlier!" I lunged forward, grabbing her arm to stop her from leaving. She slapped me hard across the face.

"Don't you ever touch me, you son of a bitch! You're lucky I don't go to the dean's office and tell her what you just did!"

She shouted in my face as I was hunched over. The thought of her telling the dean about this made my heart race. I couldn't get another strike on my record, my dad would skin me alive. "You're not going to say shit! Nothing happened, I didn't do a damn thing to you, you freaking psycho!" Her face grew red with anger, another slap caught me in the back of my head. I hadn't realized that my hand was still grasped tightly to her arm.

"We'll see what happens when everyone sees the bruise you're leaving on my arm."

She yanked her arm away, then looked down at it. I had left a visible handprint.

"Say goodbye to your future. Better hope daddy is as good of a lawyer as he expects you to be."

She turned to walk out the door, my entire future flashed before my eyes. I couldn't let this happen. Stella turned around and grabbed ahold of the door handle. I punched her as hard as I could in the back of the head. "Shit!" I cried out as her body folded on the floor at my feet. Sweat poured down my forehead, my palms started to feel moist, my heart raced faster than it ever had before. "What do I do?" I asked myself as I paced back and forth. I quickly reached down to roll Stella's unconscious body over. I reached into her pocket for the pill bottle I knew she had. "Lorazepam." I read out loud as I tuned the little orange bottle around. I opened Stella's mouth and poured the bottle in.

"What- what- are you doing?"

She came to after I had already dumped half the bottle down her throat. She coughed and gagged loudly. "Please shut up and take the damn pills!" I pleaded as I put my hand over her mouth. I didn't know how to get her to stop squirming around. I needed her to just stop so that I could think this through. A skull cracking thump echoed through my room as I slammed her head on the hardwood floor. Her eyes rolled for a moment before closing. The rest of the pills went down her throat, I put the empty bottle back into her pocket. "The tub. You took a bunch of pills, and you drowned in the tub. You were screwed up when you got here, and you got in the bath after I fell asleep." I played out the events in my head like they had actually just happened that way. I stripped her down to her bra and panties before placing her in my bathtub, I turned on the water, I watched the cold chills form all over her body.

I grabbed a black permanent marker from my desk drawer and wrote the words *'I'm sorry'* on my medicine cabinet mirror.

"Help!"

I turned to see Stella trying to sit up out of the cold water. It must have wakened her up. I ran to the side of the tub as quickly as I could, I grabbed my still wet towel from earlier off the tile floor. "Please stop!" I cried out as I scrunched the towel up and put it over her face. I shoved her back down into the water. "Please stop fighting this!" I begged and begged until her body went still in the tub. I removed the towel slowly, afraid of what she would look like as she stared up at me from the water. I crawled quickly over to the toilet and threw-up everything in my stomach. I changed clothes and climbed into my bed. As I lay there, I could still picture those bloodshot hazel eyes looking up at me.

The weeks that followed were full of confusion, not just for the school, but the police as well. My father flew in on the company jet the very next day.

"How well did you know Miss. Novak?"

"What was your relationship?"

"Did she seem depressed the night of the party?"

"Are you taking any medications?"

"The scene shows signs of struggle. Did you try to help Miss. Novak when you found her in the tub unresponsive?"

Question after question, it went on for what seemed like an eternity. I was ready to get on with my life. I was ready to move on, but no one would let me. Stella's friends and family tried to have the investigation reopened afterwards. They pushed like crazy to see me behind bars, they claimed that Stella would *'never do that to herself'*. With a little help from my father, everything went silent. A year later, I had graduated and was already interning at a firm that my father oversaw. No matter how good things got, the stress seemed to follow me like a dark cloud. It haunted me in my dreams at night. It followed me to work each morning. A month after Stella's untimely demise, I heard that her roommate Kelly had cut her wrist with a large kitchen knife. She was found dead in their room with a note that read *'It was my fault; I will never be able to live with what I have done. I can't live with this thing following me everywhere I go.'*

The school hardly noticed the string of suicides around that tim. Final exams owned the attention of the administration and every college student in the country. Life for me went on. I landed a great job that paid me the money I deserved, but no matter what I did, no matter how many pills I popped, it only seemed to slow the thing following me. Up until a few months ago, it all seemed to stop. The doctor prescribed me these miracle pills, made me focus during the day and sleep like a baby at night.

"Stella?" I asked out to the crying woman in my bathroom.

The crying stopped for a moment. I could hear the women breathing as she remained hidden around the corner. I looked over at my bedroom door. I could make it out of here if my legs and brain worked together.

"I can be whatever troubles you, David. I can be your mean old daddy who expects so much from you, I can be that office you go to everyday, or I could be the HR lady that you dread hearing from. Do you want me to be Stella? If that's what you want, I can be that."

My heart raced so fast that I could feel my chest tighten up. "I- I- I want you out- out of my fucking house!" I shouted out with a roar of defiance towards the entity. "Leave me the hell alone! Stop following me! Stop getting in my head!"

I lifted my leg and stomped my foot on the ground. "You, spiteful bitch!" My fear had evolved into anger. I was ready to face this thing. "Come out and show me your face!" I tried to make myself bigger than what I was, I had fallen prey to this thing for the last time.

"I'm coming out now, David."

The entity whispered just loud enough that I could hear.

"What- what are you?" I dropped down to my knees as the thing came around the corner to reveal itself. A lightning bolt of pain shot down my arm, my chest tightened up so tight that I couldn't catch my breath. I fell over on my side and watched the entity walk across the room towards me. I closed my eyes and hoped to die before it could touch me.

"Stress and anxiety are shape shifting entities that follow you no matter how hard you try and keep them at bay. Some are better at keeping these monsters at a distance, some foolishly let them get close enough for the kill." -Author Unknown

THE LAST OCTOBER

Salem, Kentucky
October 30th, 1989

"Jason, are you getting up today or not?"

I opened my eyes to the screech of my mother's voice coming from the kitchen downstairs. My alarm clock was knocked off the table beside my bed at some point in the night. A loud, yet satisfying pop erupted as I stretched my arms up high and yawned.

"Jason Nickey, are you going to eat this breakfast? I didn't spend all morning cooking for you to just lay there in bed."

I rolled my eyes as I laid back and pulled my pillow over my head to drown out the insufferable headache. I was nineteen years old and worked a full-time job. I deserved every wink of sleep that I could get. At the dreadful thought of my mother calling for me again, I decided it was a good time to start making some noise above her head to let her know that I was up and moving around.

"About time young man, get down her and eat!"

"I'm awake, mom. Isn't that enough?" I mumbled just low enough that she wouldn't hear. I cringed at the thought of her coming to the end of the stairs and yelling *"What did you say mister?"* Ugh, just the thought drove me nuts. I wondered if my brother Keith had heard all the yelling. Of course mother only yelled for me, wouldn't want her precious Keith missing out on any sleep. A knock at my door was the cherry on top of my proverbial shit cake. "What?" I asked pulling on my Bibliobeard amusement park t-shirt over my head.

"Open up dipshit." My idiot brother said, continuing to knock just to annoy me.

"I'm getting dressed, Dick." I responded as I pulled my ripped blue-jeans.

I checked my beard out on the crooked mirror that hung on my closet door, sucker was getting pretty long. My mother would constantly tell me how unprofessional I looked with a beard down to my chest, I reminded her that when you worked at a theme park, looking professional wasn't necessary.

"Are you going to open the door today, or are you going to keep spanking it?"

It was blatantly obvious that everyone had *pissing me off* on their agendas today. "Hold on goddamn it!" I snapped as I took my time walking over to the door. At least this prick had the common courtesy to knock, guess he would never live down walking in on his younger brother butt naked. I opened the door to see Keith leaning against the frame with that shit eating grin that he was born with plastered on his face.

"What dudes were you thinking about when you were spanking it? Hopefully not your own brother."

He laughed before slapping me hard in the chest. "Is there something you need Keith? Seeing your face first thing in the morning isn't ideal." He cocked back and laughed, I braced myself for another slap in the chest.

"Mom has been screaming for you for over ten minutes, are you going to go down there so she'll shut the hell up? Some of us need our beauty sleep. Should I call Larry and tell him that one of his employees is D-cup homo?"

I shook my head and rolled my eyes. The Larry that Keith was referring to was my boss at the park. From what I've heard, the two were close friends in high-school. Apparently Keith saved Larry from a few beat downs in the boy's locker room. Keith and I were biological brothers, only you wouldn't believe it by just looking. Keith was tall and thin, he had thick brown hair that he slicked to the side, and a freshly shaved face. Mother always said that Keith was blessed with the looks, I was blessed with creativity. I never took that as a compliment. "I'm going down there now. I'm incredibly sorry to inconvenience you, Keith. I'll make sure that Mother doesn't ever do it again." I rolled my eyes sarcastically.

"It's the day before Halloween, your favorite time of the year. Are you going to tuck your penis between your legs and wear one of mom's robes? You could be buffalo Bill when you go trick or treating."

Keith fell against the hallway wall in laughter. I just stood there waiting for him to finish. "I have to work tonight. You know what that is, right?" the laughter stopped as Keith looked at me, he was no longer amused.

"You know I'm waiting for the right offer, Dick; I'm not just going to take any old job like you. I have a little thing called self-respect. Besides, I'm only thirty-one. I still have all the time in the world. And just so you know, ass tits, I could be your supervisor at the park if I really wanted. Larry would do fucking anything for a friend like me."

He stuck his pointer finger in my face as he pursed his lips like an angry woman. "Yeah, all those jobs looking for people with a ten-year work gap. How are billion-dollar companies not knocking mom's door down trying to find you?" I could see that he was getting more and more fed-up with me, it was worth another slap.

As I entered the kitchen rubbing my bruised chest, my mother looked up at me from the table.

"You weren't being too loud up there, were you? You know how your brother gets when he hasn't had his full eight hours."

I rolled my eyes as I grabbed a plate from the cabinet. "I didn't wake up the prodigal son mom, I promise." My mother never caught on to sarcasm, which made it that much more fun.

"One day someone is going to take one good look at your brother and sign him to a big fat movie contract. I just hope he doesn't settle for any thing that comes along."

Maybe my mother *did* in fact understand sarcasm, she seemed to use it at *my* expense. From an outsider's perspective, I could see how my mom sounded like an overbearing bitch. She always had her snarky comments that she would make without making eye contact with the person she was nonchalantly insulting. My mother loved my brother and I both for different reasons, she wasn't the average nor normal mother who just loved her kids unconditionally. But, the fact that she had never laid a finger on either one of us growing up, neither did my father.

Keith and I both had great childhoods with parents who supported us in whatever endeavor.

"Are you working at that horrid place today, Nickey?"

My mother asked gesturing towards my shirt that now had a small yellow streak of egg yolk running down the front. It would make little sense to a person who didn't know my mother, but she would rather see me sit at home all day depending on her rather than me going to work. It was part of the reason that Keith is the way he is now, and always will be. "I can't just sit around the house, mom. I need to make my own money and live some semblance of a life outside these walls." I stuffed a crunchy piece of bacon in my mouth before standing up from the table.

"Well, I just don't understand what boy wouldn't want to stay home with a mother who takes care of him. I wish I knew what was so bad about being here safe at home."

I wanted so badly to sneak around the corner and run out the front door when my mother picked my plate up and walked it over to the sink. These little chats were something that I made a game out of avoiding at all costs. "I'm not a *'boy'* anymore, maw. I'm a grown man in his mid-twenties. Keith is like thirty-one. You've got to stop trying to keep us here, it's not healthy." I knew I had just lit the fuse, now I just waited for the explosion.

"What would you know about what's healthy? You work at an amusement park where all you do is push a green button to start the rollercoaster. Now you're an expert on health and parenting?"

My mother turned, tossing my empty breakfast plate into the sink. She shrugged her shoulders and mumbled something under her breath. I was out of the room before she finished. On the way to work it was impossible to keep my eyes on the road, all the Halloween decorations that filled my neighborhood made my very soul jump for joy. There was just something about fall, the leaves, the pumpkins, the cool dreary weather. It was the perfect season. I thought about what I would do this year, not much to do other than party on Halloween once you're not a kid anymore. Maybe I would hangout with Derek from work again, last year we snuck back into work after it had closed and stuffed our faces with cotton candy and leftover hotdogs. As fun as all that was, I needed something different this year.

"There he is. The wizard of shithole place." Derek called out obnoxiously as he stood atop of the picnic table that we all met at before the start of our shift. I would be embarrassed if this weren't the third time this week that he did the very same thing.

"Yeah, I'm here like always, ready to suck todays dick." I high-fived Derek as he jumped down from the picnic table. Larry the supervisor was already eyeballing us, he loved jumping on our asses the second we did something he felt wasn't "fantastic". That word alone was enough to make me want to shove a middle finger right in his nerdy face.

"Are you two boys finished with the antics? We would all really like to start this shift meeting." Larry said, pushing up his thick glasses. I looked around at my other co-workers, they all just sighed and loudly smacked their chewing gum.

"I have some super awesome news regarding Halloween here at the park. We hired our very own fortune teller!"

Larry cheered at his own announcement, unlike all of us.

"Her name is Madam Frye. She will be set up in a tent over by the goldfish booth."

A girl named Emily moaned next to me, she had been running the goldfish booth for over a year. She must have been feeling 'fantastic'. *"I don't want some weird ass lady sitting by my booth, Larry. People will be interested in something new and will be crowding all around her tent, which in turn makes them crowd around me. Put her ass somewhere else."* Emily complained, all of us laughed at her expense.

"No can do, Emily. Her tent is already set up, it's too late to move it now." Larry shrugged his shoulders and pushed his glasses back up with his pointer finger. I was curious to see this fortune teller. I wondered if she dressed like the stereotypical gypsy.

"Do you think Madam Frye is going to be hot?" Derek whispered in my ear after elbowing me in the ribs.

"Probably not, we'll check her out later." I whispered back before delivering an elbow of my own. Larry said something else that I wasn't paying any attention to as every dispersed. I looked over at the roller coaster I had been working at for the last two years. The fact that the damn thing hadn't collapsed was a modern miracle.

"Poseidon"

I walked under the big, faded letters painted on the archway, and up the stairs to my two-by-three-foot booth. I leaned back as far as my chair would allow me. Hopefully Derek would be put up here to check seatbelts. Knowing Larry, that wouldn't happen. I looked over at the train of cars lined up on the old wooden tracks, it sat there cold and lifeless, just waiting to fulfill its only purpose.

"I'm assuming you're about to do the test run." A voice coming from the stairs startled the hell out of me. I looked over to see Trisha walking over towards my booth.

Trisha was about my age and had been working here for as long as I had. She was the only African American women that I had ever seen work at this park, she was also the prettiest. I kicked myself in the ass almost everyday for not growing the balls to ask her out. Guess I didn't see myself as much of a catch for a beautiful woman like Trisha.

"Yeah, I was just about to. What are you doing up here, don't you work the bumper cars?" I asked, trying to make conversation any way that I could. Why bother? I was a carny that lived at home with his parents and unemployable older brother. What did I have to offer?

"Larry told me to come up here and help you today, figured it would be fun considering in all the time I've been here I've never worked on the tallest ride in the park."

She smiled as she looked over the edge and down at the ground way below. I was overly excited that Trisha would be working up here today. Maybe this day wouldn't be as monotonous as I assumed. "Well, welcome to the top of the world. You finally made it." We laughed together before doing the Poseidon's daily safety test and walk-through, a rickety piece of scrap wood and steel, as always.

"Have you had the chance to meet that new fortune teller yet?" Trisha asked as we began unlocking the gates.

"No, not yet. Why? is she weird?" I wondered if Trisha would be offended by my question. Maybe she didn't like talking shit behind someone's back, I now looked like that type of person.

"Well, she's a tad strange looking. She's blind, so both eye's are this creepy light grey. Her hair is white and super frizzy, like bride of Frankenstein frizzy."

I felt a wave of relief after hearing Trisha say that the fortune teller looked strange. I now knew I could speak openly. "Couldn't look as bad as Larry. She's lucky she didn't have to look at his little mustache during the interview." We both cracked up so loudly, we didn't realize that people had started lining up at the top of the steps. The day went great with Trisha helping out, I showed her my little red and green buttons, she kindly pretended to find them fascinating. For the first time at this job, I found myself not wanting my day to end. I would have pulled a double with Trisha if that were possible.

"What would you say to hanging out after work sometime?" Trisha asked as I locked my booth.

I nearly dropped my keys. "Um, yeah, that would be awesome. If we go on a date, I promise not to bring you here." I laughed awkwardly as I felt this was the one thing I would say to ruin everything. Surprisingly, she smiled and jokingly shrugged.

"Let me get to see Jason Nickey the man first, I've only seen Jason Nickey the carny. You could turn out to be a total bore outside of this place."

She nudged me and laughed. This was unequivocally, without question, the best day I had ever had at work. "Should I get your number or something? I guess I wouldn't really need it considering we see each other every day." As cool as Trisha was, I kept questioning the things I asked or said. I had some serious undiagnosed self-esteem issues.

"I'll give you my number. If you call and my dad answers, don't show any weaknesses. He'll smell your fear from a mile away." She laughed and rolled her eyes.

"You still live with your parents?" I asked surprised and slightly relieved.

"Yeah, just my dad, he's not very keen on me growing up anytime soon."

Was this the most perfect girl in the world? Was I dreaming this entire day? Would I wake up to Keith's balls dangling in my face? A day that started out like a shit sandwich had blossomed into a beautiful butterfly, as little sense as that made.

"Bro, have you seen that fortune teller? She's fucking freaky looking, might be just your type."

I lowered my head and wished I could crawl into my beard and hide. Hoping to not cross paths with Derek when leaving was a longshot. His timing was impeccable. "I heard she looked strange, Derek. Thank you for the update." I said, rolling my eyes for a moment before looking over hoping Trisha had zoned so far out that she didn't hear anything around her.

"I'm sorry I got Larry pissed enough that he didn't send you any help. I would have snuck up there if I had known you were all by yourself, shit had to be dull.""

"I had help, genius." I motioned over at Trisha who was still walking without paying any attention to Derek.

"That's hilarious. Want to drive me home tonight, might let you jerk me off."

I slapped Derek's chest with the back of my hand. "How rude do you plan on being?" I asked as he rubbed his chest and looked over at me with biggest shit eating grin I had ever seen.

"Did you get some chicks number today? Was she as hot as your mom?"

I rolled my eyes. Did Derek have beef with Trisha? She must have turned him down at some point, only explanation for him not acknowledging her. "I have shit to do, have your stepmom pick you up." I slapped at him again, but he was able to dodge it.

"Suck my tits."

He laughed as he gave me the middle finger, then scurried off like a mouse that had just got away with a piece of cheese. I looked over at Trisha, who was standing with her arms crossed, staring at me with the shit eating grin that she must have just learned from Derek. "What?" I asked looking around like I assumed she was looking at something else.

"Derek is quite the character. I have friends just like him outside of work, they always seem to say the worst things at even worse times. Don't be embarrassed, Jason. My opinion of you isn't going to change at Derek's expense."

I shrugged with a goofy smile "Well, if you say so." We laughed together for a moment before a high pitched scream cut through the cool fall air. "What in the hell was that?" I asked, trying to pinpoint the location of the scream. Trisha looked around as well, neither of us could tell where it was coming from. Then, like before, the same terrified scream pierced the silence around us. "Where in the hell is that coming from?" I started to become frustrated, then we saw the source of the screaming.

"Emily?" Trisha and I asked each other at the exact same time. We shot our gaze over towards the goldfish booth. Emily was running from the new fortune teller tent, tears streaming down her petrified face.

"She knows how I'm going to die. How the fuck can she know that?!"

Trisha and I looked at each other and then back at Emily, who was now running in our direction. "Emily, what happened?" I asked, trying to stop her. She dodged my out reached arms like a pro basketball player.

"Emily, wait!" Trisha called out as she was about to give chase, she stopped after a few steps.

"What was that all about? She said something about her dying. Maybe the fortune teller told her something she didn't like hearing. Only someone like Emily would fall for some cheap parlor trick."

Trisha and I found ourselves laughing together for the millionth time today.

"My truth comes cheap, but a trick it most certainly is not."

"Holy shit!" I cried out, almost falling into Trisha. An old women with frizzy white hair and pale grey eyes stood only feet from us. "How the hell did you sneak up on us like that lady? You scared the shit out of us." I said holding my chest and smiling over at Trisha.

"I am Madam Frye, but you knew that already. No time to waste on small talk, come and have your fortune read, free of charge."

I looked over at Trisha, expecting her to butt in with an answer that would get us out of this without having to follow the creepy old lady to her tent.

"We'd love to!"

Well, so much for an escape plan. Trisha and I followed the old lady towards her tent. It was red and white striped, like an old-time circus tent, a purple light shown through the draped open entrance way. The old women looked like some voodoo doctor I had seen on an old movie, she had this Cajun accent that I had actually never heard from someone in person. I felt Trisha nudge me as we followed behind the old women, she covered her nose.

"What is that smell?" She whispered quietly, hoping the old lady wouldn't hear.

"The smell is the sage I burn, not the best smelling stuff."

The old lady said stopping to look back at Trisha. Trisha's eyes now like saucers as she looked over at me with her face stretched out like she had just taken a big chomp out of her tongue. "I don't mean any disrespect, but how is it that you knew there were two of us, and where you were going?" Trisha nudged me with her elbow while shaking her head in disapproval.

"I can see better than most. You see the world with more than a set of eyes, the world looks how you want to see it."

I couldn't make sense of the old women's riddle, it didn't answer how she was so good at finding her way around an area that she had only been around for a few hours. Maybe the blind thing was an act, maybe this how getup was part of her act. If so, she was good at it. We entered the tent, the smell of the old women's sage was even stronger inside, it gave me a headache after only a few seconds. There were animal bones hanging from the ceiling, shelves around the walls lined with jars of things I couldn't quite make out. A table sat in the middle of the floor, a purple and gold trimmed cloth draped over it.

"No crystal ball, how are you supposed to see the future?" I asked side eyeing Trisha to see if she thought it was funny, she just stood there, looking up at the hanging bones.

"I never said I was going to read your future, boy. Madam Frey am not into all that palm reading non-sense, only truth be told here."

Oddly, her accent grew thicker. She must have been getting into character, guess she forgot outside. I laughed, patting Trisha on the arm hoping she had noticed the change. She looked over at me like her soul had just evacuated her body. I could see the cold chills forming on her bare arms. "What's wrong?" I asked concerningly.

"Ain't no concern to you now, boy. Take a seat and let's get to it now."

I ignored the old lady as she rummaged for something under the table. I didn't feel right about being here. I could tell Trisha felt the same way. "We can go, if you're not feeling up to this." I whispered close to her ear with no response. "Look, Miss Frye, I think we're just going to go. My friend isn't feeling to well. We'll stop by some other time." I tried guiding Trisha to the exit but she wouldn't budge. "Let's get out of here, lets get you home. I'll drive you if you want." Trisha just stared up at the animal bones that rattled like creepy windchimes.

"You like dat Halloween don't ya boy? Well, you'll like what I got for ya."

The fortune teller laid what appeared to be a human skull in the middle of the table. My skin crawled like I had just stepped into a giant ant hill. "Is that a real human skull?" I asked, taking a step towards the table. The old women just nodded and gestured for me to sit down. I absolutely loved Halloween, there was no question about it. I've been watching horror movies and obsessing about writing my own horror novel for who knows how long. I leaned more towards the bizarre than most people I knew, but something was far too creepy about this. I pulled out one of the chairs from the small table. I looked down between my legs in hesitation knowing that a human skull was just pulled from under said table.

"No need to worry your head boy, no rattling bones going to get cha under there."

This creepy old lady seemed to know everything I was thinking before even I had the chance to think it. I looked up at Trisha who was now walking towards one of the shelves that had a vast number of jars filled with a murky liquid. Maybe she was starting to come around. "So, what can you tell about me by looking at that skull?" I asked almost wanting to reach out and feel it (out of morbid curiosity)

"I got this skull just for you, boy. Knew it was the one you needed. Seems its been doing a good job at keepin ya company today. Only works this time a year, lucky for you."

I didn't understand what the hell the old lady was going on about, I was almost afraid to ask. "So, what can you tell me? Am I going to get lucky and win the lottery one of these days?" I said trying to lighten the grim vibe. Madam Frye looked up at me, obviously not as amused as I was.

"She can stay with ya until All-hallowmas has come to an end. After dat, I'm needin' her back now. Ya hear me, boy?"

If I were able to make out anything coming from this lady's mouth, it would have made this situation a little more tolerable, but right then, I just wanted to go. "I don't really understand what you mean, Madam Frye. You may have to dumb it down for me a bit, I didn't pay much attention in voodoo 101." (If there were such a thing, I would have paid attention)

"This here skull belonged to me daughter, she done died over forty years ago. Had got that pneumonia, died at only nineteen."

"That is your daughters fucking skull? What the hell lady, you just carry that around and show it to strangers?" I asked, ready to get up. I looked over at Trisha. I hoped she was ready to bounce as much as I was. "Trisha, we need to go. This lady has her daughter's skull sitting on the table and shit."

"You watch your mouth around me daughter, boy. I'll not have you cussing like some heathen. I gave ya a gift, now return it at midnight on what you call Halloween."

"A gift? What gift are you talking about? If you think I'm about to walk out of here with that skull, you're even more batshit crazy than I thought." I went to stand up, but Madam Frye pounded her fists on the table.

"Sit yourself down, boy. I aint playin no games wit ya. Me daughters name was Trisha, Trisha Frye. She the one you keep lookin at. I sent her to ya because you respect the true meaning of All-Hallowmas, not like this folks out disrespecting the traditions. It means something to ya boy."

As morbid as it sounds, I couldn't help but start laughing. I had been taken for a ride. Madam Frye stared at me confused. I looked over at Trisha, I waited for her to take a bow. I commended her dedication to the prank. "I'm guessing you two talked before Larry sent you over to me today. Wee Larry and Derek in on it too? If so, I must give them serious props." Trisha just stood there staring at Madam Frye, only Madam Frye never looked at her.

"This ain't no joke, Jason. The girl you be seein' is me daughter, Trisha. She was one of the most kind-hearted people anyone ever knew, only those dat are truly alone, can see me daughter the way she is now. You take this bag, I put the skull in, you return it like I say. Show me daughter the respect she done deserves now."

I truly did appreciate a good joke. I spent at least three hours of everyday just thinking about creative pranks to pull on people, but this was going a bit over the top. "Trisha?" I asked reaching for the skull in the middle of the table. "Does this belong to you?" I asked, holding it towards her. Kept my goofy expression to show that I hadn't fallen for the ruse.

"It's mine, Jason. I'm sorry I couldn't tell you before, all this time and I still forget until I start smelling that sage. That damn stuff makes a flood of memories come pouring in all at once and it's difficult to accept that you're dead."

The sincerity that I felt from her made me ditch the goofy look. "Look, this is all some kind of joke. The sage must have messed with your head. I know it's a joke because I've known you way before this crazy old lady ever showed up. You've worked here for as long as I have." I looked back over at Madam Frye; I was curious if she could explain her way around that one.

"Dem not real memories, boy. You the only one that can see her, no one else."

I thought for a moment about the day I had just spent working with Trisha, someone had to have said something to her or acknowledged her in some capacity. Shit, even Derek didn't seem to notice her. I looked over at Trisha, and then back at Madam Frye. "This isn't a joke?" I asked as my voice cracked. Madam Frye just shook her head and handed me a brown burlap sack.

"Return the skull to me on midnight tomorrow ya hear? Not a minute later. There be serious consequences if you be late, or you show disrespect to me daughter. Member boy, only the most alone in dis world can see or hear me daughter now. Be careful who ya bring around. And just so ya know, I use me daughter's skull for good. I have others, not so much."

I handed the skull back to Madam Frye. She placed it inside the sack, tying it with some old rope.

"You might come out dis a new person. Member boy, it's a gift."

I took the sack and tucked it under my arm, I felt Trisha grab me hand as we walked out of the tent. The further towards the parking lot we got, the more the old Trisha started coming back.

"What a day, I had fun though. I think I'll ask if I can work with you from now on."

I smiled at her, but under my smile was the worst sadness that I had ever felt. "So, where to?" I asked extremely curious as to what her response would be considering she didn't actually live anywhere.

"Well, we can't go back to my house. My dad would flip out if I brought a guy home. I'll call him from your house and say that I'm hanging out with some girlfriends from work. If it's cool that I come hangout at your place."

She placed her hand on my shoulder as we buckled our seatbelts. "Yeah, sure. We can go hangout at my place, my parents won't mind. We'll just avoid everyone all together. I can introduce you to them at some other time." Trisha lit up with excitement, it was like she just won the new car on the price is right. I wanted to be happy, I wanted to cherish this moment. All I felt was gut wrenching sadness.

"What's in the creepy old bag? You have a human head in there that you're not telling me about?"

I almost choked on my own spit. "Um, it's just some stuff from my booth at work, didn't want to lose any of it." I lied as Trisha rolled down the passenger's side window to hold her hand out, the wind blowing between her fingers made a calming *woosh* sound. I couldn't stop looking over at her as my mind fought to understand her very existence.

"Are you so excited that tomorrow is Halloween? I wish we were young enough to trick or treat. I could really go for a pillowcase full of candy."

I wondered to myself how many Halloweens Trisha had seen. Did her Mother hand out her fucking skull to some lonely loser like me every year? How many people like me had she come to know just to forget them? I felt like there were heavy weights pressing down on my shoulders. I didn't have the time to adjust mentally to this. We pulled into my driveway, the headlights of my car beamed off the two trashcans that sat in front of the garage door. "This is it." I said as I put the car in park. "It's a pretty decent neighborhood, not a lot of crime or anything like that." Trisha looked over at me with a smile, then back at the house.

"It's definitely you." She said, jokingly. I shook my head in amusement as I walked around to open her door.

"What a gentleman, didn't think carnies knew how to be so proper."

"Well, I do run the classiest ride at the park. Maybe it's rubbed off on me."

We both laughed, only my laughter was cut short by the fact that we had to walk into my house. It would make this so much easier if only Trisha knew about herself. I hoped like hell that everyone was sound asleep. Knowing my mother, she was probably camped out on the recliner in the living room, just waiting for me to walk in the door.

"Did you carve these?"

My train of thought was broken by Trisha admiring the jack-o-lanterns I had carved and put out on the porch, my mother must have put candles in them earlier. "Yeah, you like them?" I asked, already knowing she wasn't going to tell me that they sucked and that I should stick to pushing buttons.

"I love them. I love everything about Halloween, it's the perfect time of year."

It felt like she had taken my thoughts and feelings and ran with them. "I couldn't agree more. Everything about this time of year is so alluring." I looked up at the starless night sky, the dark clouds allowed the moon to peak out ever so much. "Would you want to go on a walk with-

"Hey, dick breath. Who's the chick? Or is that really dude dressed up like a chick? Knowing you, I choose the latter."

I looked up to see Keith leaning out of his bedroom window. I hoped he had pants on.

Wait, holy shit, Keith could see Trisha. "This is Trisha. We work together. She's going to hangout with me for a little while. Now fuck off and get back to doing full all." I felt a wet splat land on top of my head. Keith's spit rolled down my forehead and into my eye.

"Bullseye bitch!"

Keith slammed his window shut; I could hear him laughing hysterically at my expense. Trisha pulled her shirt up slightly and wiped the spit form my face. "Thanks for that." I said feeling like a complete pussy.

"No problem. I'm sure having an older brother can be a bit challenging at times."

"You don't know the half of it. Now, like I was trying to ask before the king of nothing interrupted. Would you like to go on a walk? We will pass by the cemetery, it's eerie this late at night." Trisha turned to look down the road, then back at my house.

"As awesome as a dark cemetery sounds, I think we should go to your room and take a rest on your bed. I'm sure you have a shirt I can wear, I don't want your brothers spit on me all night."

Trisha seemed desperate to get upstairs. I knew it wasn't my charm or good looks that seemed to compel her. Why was she so eager to go in the house? I mean, I wasn't complaining that some really hot chick that I would never see again wanted to give me the time of my life. Occasionally, I just remind myself that if something seems too good to be true, it probably is. "Are you sure that your dad isn't going to get a little suspicious and come looking for you? I just don't want to be the reason you get into any trouble." Speaking of suspicion, that was the look I received after asking that question.

"Is there something up, Jason? Do you not want me in your house or something?"

I pretended to be offended by the accusation "Um, of course I want you in my house. What in the world would make you think that? I was just looking out for you. I don't want to stir up any trouble with your father." Her left eyebrow stayed raised for a moment, it was like she was trying to read me. She then smiled and turned to look up at my bedroom window.

"Well Jason Nickey, show me inside."

She gestured towards the front door. My stomach was in knots picturing my mother waking up and questioning my whereabouts. "Well, alright, lets go." I led the way through the small iron gate and up to the front porch. I tried to nonchalantly look through the downstairs windows without Trisha knowing I was doing so. I stuck my key into the deadbolt, then finally opening the door. Downstairs was dark, quiet, and seemingly uninhabited by an interrogating mother. "Let's head upstairs, my door is at the end of the hall." I let Trisha ascend first, my mind still all over the place, this whole think with Madam Frye couldn't be real, she never *proved* anything.

"Which one is your brothers?"

Trisha looked around curiously as we tiptoed down the dimly lit hallway. I wondered why it even mattered. "It's right there, lets try to not disturb his majesty." Trisha stopped for a few moments in front of Keith's door, then continued down towards mine.

"Is that your parents' room down at the other end? Are they heavy sleepers?"

I turned and looked down at the closed door at the other end of the hall, I pictured my mother with those stupid looking pink rolls in her hair, snoring so loud that the headboard vibrated. "My mom wouldn't even wake up to you smashing her kneecaps with a Louisville slugger bat. My dad is on some teambuilding retreat his job sent him to, he is supposed to be back on Friday. I don't think we're going to have to worry about him." Trisha giggled quietly as I opened the door to my bedroom. I couldn't remember exactly how I had left it earlier, obviously I didn't picture anything like *this* happening.

"Nice posters. This place is totally you." Trisha said, nodding with her hands on her hips.

How did she know that my room suited me? Was she under the impression the way that I was, did she think that she had known me before today? "Yeah, it's kind of a mess right now. I didn't expect company in this lifetime." I reached down to throw a pair of two-day-old underwear behind my dresser. I put the brown sack containing what I was told was Trisha's skull next to my closet door. "What kind of music do you like? I think we talked about that earlier, but got distracted." Trisha looked around at all the heavy metal bands that were wallpapered around my tiny bedroom.

"I'm not very familiar with any of these groups, seems too heavy for my tastes."

I wondered if Trisha even remembered any of the bands of her time. I mean, if she died as long ago as Madam Frye said that she had, I wouldn't be surprised if she didn't listen to smooth jazz or something similar. "So, what do you want to do? I have some good VHS tapes. I have two sets of headphones if you want to listen to some music." I looked around for the headphones, but was stopped by Trisha taking off her shirt.

"I had something else in mind."

She said seductively as she walked closer towards me. Her bra was black and silky, her perfectly toned stomach made me feel slightly self-conscious. I tried looking into her eyes, but her breasts jiggled with every step that she drew closer. "Well, um, alright." My mouth grew dry, and my palms became wet and clammy. I had only had sex once before, it was like six or seven years ago with a customer at the park. It wasn't nearly as romantic as this situation seemed. It was in a porta-potty behind the Ferris wheel, it lasted a total of three minutes. What if I'm a three-minute man? Holy shit, that would be an embarrassing waste of the precious little time I had left with Trisha.

"Take off your clothes and get in bed."

Trisha nodded over to my un-made bed in the corner of the room. I would have preferred to take off my clothes in the heat of the moment, like in the movies, they barely looked at each other during the removal of clothing. But here I was, standing naked with my hands over my dick. Damn, I'm going to walk past her, and she is going to have to look at my pastey white ass. I walked backwards towards the bed instead, she laughed as she knew why I was doing so.

"Would you feel better if I showed you mine?"

Trisha unbuttoned her jeans, they dropped down to her ankles. "Holy shit!" I think I said out loud as I gazed upon the greatness that stood before me. Trisha's black panties matched her bra, it looked so good against her light, caramel skin. Her ass was heart-shaped, the panties rode up high enough that they left nothing to the imagination. I now laid on my bed, completely exposed, hard as a rock.

"Play with yourself Jason. Stoke it for me, make me want it."

Trisha begged as she bit down on her bottom lip. Once again, it wasn't something I would have preferred, but what the hell. I started stroking my penis, I wondered what she thought of it, I also wondered how in the hell I was turning her on right now. My eye's rolled back, I needed her on the bed so badly, she rubbed her hands down her chest as she continued biting her lip.

"Now!" she shouted with a huge smile and turning quickly to my bedroom door.

"Gotcha Dick jacket!"

Keith rushed through the door with his camera, he took three shots before I even had a chance to cover myself. "What in the fuck are you doing, Keith. Get the hell out of here!" I looked over at Trisha as she and Keith wrapped arms around one another, laughing and pointing at me. I grabbed my blanket and covered myself, I felt completely humiliated.

"Goddamn baby, you played that shit good! I didn't think it was going to work, even on this total dumbass. But here you all are, brown bag and all!"

Keith reached down, grabbing the burlap sack containing the skull. I felt at least three separate emotions at once. None of them favorable.

"You have to give it up to Larry and my grandma as well, I couldn't have pulled that shit off without them. Hell, Keith, even Jason's dumbass friend Derek went along with it after I promised to flash him later."

Keith and Trisha laughed even harder. Keith pulled the skull out of the bag and gave it a kiss before tossing it at me.

"I knew my brother was gullible, but I didn't know he was completely retarded. How in the world did you fall for that bullshit that Trisha's grandma sold you? She doesn't even do a good fake Cajun accent. And you've worked with Trisha like every fucking day at that shitty job. How are you so stupid, bro?"

I felt my eye's start to burn, this was the absolute worst time to start crying. "I- I- fuck the both of you! Why would you pull this shit on me? What the hell did I do to deserve it?!" I asked as I aggressively pulled my pants and underwear back on. "A girl shows some interest in me, and of course, it's a big fucking joke." I had never felt so angry in my life. This was low, even for someone like Keith. "You got my fucking boss and co-workers in on this shit, Keith? Larry didn't suck your dick enough in high school, so he does this little favor for you?" Keith looked over at Trisha, his smile faded as his forehead turned a shade of red.

"You are always talking shit to me about not having a job and being a loser. I wanted to teach your smug ass a lesson. Trisha's grandma starting at the fair today and tomorrow being Halloween was just too perfect. Sorry you can't take a joke, you big cry baby."

I ignored Keith as I looked over at Trisha. She pulled her shirt and pants back on before making eye contact with me. "What was in this for you? Why did you do this shit to me?" I asked putting my shirt on as well.

"She did it be-

"Shut the fuck up, Keith. I didn't ask you. I asked this lying bitch what she got off it!" The look I gave Keith was enough that he looked over and waited on Trisha's response without uttering another word.

"Where do you get off calling me a bitch, asshole? I did it because Keith asked me too, plus it felt nice to get back at the pervert piece of shit who fucked my teenage sister in a fucking porta-potty! Yeah, dumbfuck, not many of us black folks in this cracker ass town, did it not occur to you that the few of us that live here might be related somehow?"

"I didn't want to assume that you two were related because that would be kind of racist, don't you think? I didn't know it was your sister, and even if I did, what the hell does it matter?" I asked getting more and more angry. "Did I beat the shit out of her afterwards? Did we exchange numbers and I not call her? Or is it that you wished it had been *you* getting fucked over a shit hole?"

Trisha opened her mouth to respond, but all our eyes darted to my still opened bedroom door.

"What in the world are you boy's doing up this late, being so freaking loud?"

My groggy eyed mother stood in the doorway wearing a white bathrobe, it took her a moment before she was awake enough to realize that it wasn't just Keith and I.

"I'm sorry, who might you be? Are you Keith's girlfriend he's been going on and on about?"

Of course my mother would jump straight to assuming this pretty girl was Keith's girlfriend. I guess she expected some mammoth with a double chin to be hiding naked in my closet.

"Oh, yeah. I'm Trisha, it's so nice to finally meet you. Sorry I couldn't make a better first impression Mrs. Nickey."

I rolled my eyes at Trisha's fake attempt at sincerity, she must have taken acting lessons from her con-artist grand-mother.

"Nonsense, it would be a pleasure to meet you no matter what time it was. I'm so glad that my Keith has found someone so well mannered, hopefully it rubs off on him."

The three of them laughed as I sat in the background, my fist's clenched tightly. "Is this part of the fucking joke as well? You get mom in on your bullshit?" I asked so viciously that spit flew from my lips. "I guess your perfect little asshole didn't plan on telling you about the elaborate prank that he and this bitch pulled on me today." My mothers' face went from happy, to shocked beyond belief.

"Jason Nickey! You watch your mouth, I don't ever want to hear talk like that under this roof. Now you apologize to your brother and Trisha. A little joking around with your sibling is nothing to get angry over, you are a grown man, start acting like it!"

My mother snapped her fingers at me, her eye's wide with embarrassment.

"I am so very sorry about that Trisha. Jason doesn't have many friends so he lashes out on his brother who has lots of them. I always tell him to hang around Keith a little more and learn how to talk to people."

Trisha turned to me with a smile that my mother couldn't see.

"It's alright, maybe with a little time he'll learn to grow up and take a joke."

I clenched my jaw so tight that I felt one of my back teeth split open. I watched as my brothers entourage piled out of my room until I stood there alone, alone and fed-up.

"It's midnight little bro, happy Halloween!"

Keith called out from his bedroom as he and Trisha laughed about what they had done. I looked down at the burlap sack and skull that lay on my bedroom floor. I smiled, remembering that I needed to return the skull to Madam Frye. After all, it was now Halloween.

My alarm clock went off right beside my face, I reached up with my eye's still closed and smacked it until it shut off. I sat up and stretched as I forced myself out from under my warm covers. I felt a charge of energy as I looked out from my bedroom window, and out on to the sidewalk covered in dead leaves. I couldn't help but smile, it was my favorite day of the year, and this, this would be the best one yet.

I got up and pulled my work shirt over my head, I reached down and grabbed the brown sack that now sat atop my dresser. There was no smell of bacon and eggs filling the house on this Halloween morning, just a beautiful silence that I had never heard before. I walked down past Keith's room, the door wide open for the first time ever this early in the day. Keith's bloody corpse lay on his bed, his intestines ripped out and draped neatly around his bedroom. I smiled as the sight reminded me of the

Halloween decorations I would see throughout town on my way to work. Down the hall my parents' door was opened as well, that was no surprise, as my mom liked to wake up at the crack of dawn. It was nice that she would be taking a break from cooking today, her throat slashed from a broken piece of bathroom mirror, my dad would come home to find his wife of thirty-two years, hunched over the bathtub to bleed out. I looked at my hands, the blood was so thick that when it dried it felt like hardened mud. A shower wouldn't be necessary today, many necessities of everyday life seemed bleak and gratuitous. I looked myself over; using the shattered mirror that covered the hallway floor. Like the broken glass, I was a splintered reflection of my former self, no longer did I see Jason Nickey looking back at me.

"Fuck you mother-fuckers!" I screamed at the top of my lungs as I used the giant shard of glass to make my face scary for the last Halloween. The adrenaline pumping through my veins kept the agonizing pain that I should be feeling at bay. Chunks of my face splatted loudly on the pile of broken mirror.

"Fuck you!" I screamed so hard that I could feel the cuts in my face split open even wider. I headed down the steps and out the front door, the cool air felt good against my burning face. I through the sack into the back seat as my neighbors started to notice the new Halloween decorations I worked all night putting up. I heard them all whispering amongst themselves, I saw two children turn their heads and bury their faces deep into their mothers' stomach. I took one last look at my decorations before driving away. Trisha's nude, headless body, hung from the balcony, a human skull was shoved deep into a gash on her abdomen, the word *'Bitch'* carved crudely down her bare thigh. I knew the neighbors would call the police, they would think it was either a prank call or someone's Halloween decorations looked *too* real. Eventually they would show up and find all the bodies. I knew they would find me at the park that I spent almost every waking moment of my life at. They would climb the never- ending steps of the roller-coaster, aim their guns, tell me to freeze. It would all be pointless because I would throw myself over the railing, inevitably falling to my death. Hopefully I had time to return this sack to Madam Frye, hopefully she doesn't mind that I put a new head in it.

"Karma has no menu. You get served what you deserve."
-Author unknown

I'll Bury You Tomorrow

Bateman County, California

June 15ᵗʰ, 1979

A loud crack let me know that her neck had snapped. All that fight that she had given me had now come to a complete stop. I felt the weight when her body fell limp in my arms. "Fuck me. That could've gone a little better."

I laid the girl's body on the edge of the in-ground pool, the water was so green and disgusting. It would be a good hiding spot for the next few days until I was able to bury the body proper. "What did you say your name was?" I asked, tilting the girls head to get a look at her face. Her eyes were bloodshot, her mouth hung open, and drool dripped down her pale chin. Before tying one end of a three-foot long rope around her neck, and the other end around a fifty-pound dumbbell, I looked at her once more. It was sad that we had more in common than I cared to admit. I watched as her body flopped like a rag doll as it hit the thin layer of slime that rested on top of the stagnate pool water. "It sure sucks that you weren't good enough to be with the rest of them. I'll find you a decent hole tomorrow." I turned and walked back to the house.

"A severe weather alert has been issued for Bateman County. All residents are asked to stay indoors. Hurricane Otis is expected to hit at-

I shut the Tv off before checking my hair in the mirror. I reached in the small glass of water to get my 'company teeth'. They fit right over the rotted black ones. My face was applied perfectly. I looked very presentable, not that it mattered in this case.

"Ding Dong"

"I'm guessing you're the girl that the agency sent." I smirked as I opened the door to a beautiful young woman in a short red dress. I licked my lips as my eye's studied every inch of her body. "I thought they were going to send me another six, looks like they went with an eight. Lucky me."

I could tell the escort was appalled by my prickish demeaner. I couldn't care-less. I didn't need her respect, she didn't need mine. I watched her head move at every angle as she studied my magnificent home, she was only seconds from asking what I did for a living. I didn't want to grow bored from small talk.

"Wow, your home is so beautiful. What is it that-"

"Let me stop you right there, sweetheart." I put my hand up to silence her. "Let's not do this small talk. I own a very successful business which provides me with enough disposable income to buy this house and anything else that I want. *You* are a whore who fucks rich guys like me for an absurd amount of money. You are not here to talk with that mouth. You are here to suck my dick with it, if I feel you are worth it."

The young escort just stood there chewing on a wad of minty smelling chewing gum. Just as I thought, dumb as a fucking rock. "Now come in, take off those cheap high-heels, and spit that annoying ass gunk that's slopping around in your mouth in those bushes to your right." The escort did as she was told without question. Though I would never admit it out loud, this whore was almost a solid ten in the looks department. Her long blonde hair, her blue eye's like small diamonds, her perfect little body in that fucking dress. Another thing I wouldn't be admitting out loud was that I was a serial killer who had already dispatched eight other whores just this week, in this very house. She would eventually find out. I mean, she would know very well when my hands are around her skinny little neck, and I watch those blue eyes turn bloodshot and grey. She would beg like all the others. She would tell me she had a family and kids. All the same bullshit.

"Do you work out? You look like you do."

I rolled my eyes as I opened a cheap bottle of the champagne I left out for the less intriguing guests. Obviously she was checking out my body. I was built like a brick fucking wall, my half unbuttoned white dress shirt looked as if it were painted on. I was a fucking stallion, big dick, big house, bigger bank account. I turned and looked at the women who now sat on my leather couch. She stared up at me as I handed her a champagne filled glass.

"Oh, sorry. I don't drink. I'm eight-months sober as of yesterday. It was this whole thing with getting to keep my son-"

"Just shut the fuck up. Are you new at this? Do you not know how this shit works? I don't want to hear about some kid that you popped out of the snatch that I'm about to have my cock in. And secondly, you will fucking drink my champagne because I fucking offered it to you. It's called having fucking manners." I could feel that I was red-faced, my hand squeezing the glass hard enough to smash it. "Take the glass or hit the bricks with nothing to show for it." I reached the glass out to her once more, she took it with a forced smile. The moment that her fingers grazed mine, I knew I wanted to take her apart, piece by piece.

"I apologize, sir. You are my first classy customer. I didn't mean to offend you."

I scoffed at her apology. "You think *you* could offend *me*?" I asked, growing more and more tired of this conversation. Like a hungry dog, I wanted nothing more than to fucking eat. "You couldn't offend me if you tried. What could you possibly say that would offend me? You have nothing in this world but a lack of alcohol and a snot nosed brat that you can hardly take care of."

I pulled the twenty-five-hundred dollars out of my front pocket. I fanned it, I smelt it, I fucking flaunted it. "This is the money that you could be walking out of here with. I know you'll get just enough of it from your fucking pimp just to keep the lights on in the shitty apartment you live in. How about this. I'll throw in an extra thousand, off the record." I watched those blue eyes light up. I was so close to having her in tears just a few moments ago. This was where the fun always started. Get them worked up, get them feeling every emotion, it's so much more satisfying when they've been through the ringer. "I'll give you a thousand more dollars. You pocket whatever that prick pimp gives you, plus the extra thousand. How does that sound?" she almost came off the couch in excitement. I could tell right then and there, she would do anything I asked.

"Do you want me to suck your cock? I can do any position you want. I'll even put something in your ass, if you like that kind of thing."

I shook my head feeling the same level of annoyed as I felt when I heard the chomping of that fucking chewing gum. "You dumb bitch. You're already supposed to do any sexual shit I ask for, that's what you're here for. This extra money is for special things." I flopped the money around by her face. She looked up at me bewildered.

"Oh, um, okay. Like silly stuff? Like do you want to take pictures or record a video of us fucking? That's usually not allowed, but for extra, I'm down."

I couldn't believe how dense this girl was. Did her pimp pay her in fucking compliments? "I'll show you exactly what will land you this extra money" I said, walking over to the kitchen entrance. I returned with a pair of pliers I had snagged from my junk drawer. "I want you to take these." I handed her the pliers. She looked at them as confused as I imagined she would be. "I want you to start ripping off those godawful nails. The color is just atrocious." She looked up at me again, this time a little less *confused,* and a little more afraid.

"I could just use some fingernail polish remover and take the color off that way. These are my real nails so I-"

I put my hand up again to shut her mouth. She obviously took me for a dumbass. "I'm very aware that they are your real nails, and for that you should be embarrassed. They are hideous in color, and length. I want them taken off in the next five minutes, or you can kiss this extra thousand goodbye." She looked back down at the pliers, then back up at me. She was like a baby antelope cornered by a blood thirsty lion. "Your time starts now, sweetie. Get to it. If you decide that you don't want the extra money, just tell me now. I'll toss it in the fireplace and you can just spread your legs for peanuts." I walked over to the roaring fireplace with a wad of hundreds in hand. Her eyes grew like she was about to watch her own child be burned alive.

"Please, don't. I'll do what you asked!"

She started sobbing. Either she wanted my sympathy, or she just craved looking like an unattractive pig. "Stop all that fucking crying. It's disgusting!" I was getting more and more tired of her stupidity. I tossed the money into the roaring fire.

"Wait! I said I would do it!"

The back of my neck was hot enough to cook a ten-ounce ribeye. This was the exact reason I had no issue killing these stupid whores, it was clear that they could never contribute to society. "I told you to take off those nails, not sit there and sob like a fucking baby. You didn't do as I asked, so now you can get fucked!" The extent of my rage made the escort move further back onto the couch. She wrapped her arms around herself like a scared child.

"Please, sir. I could really use that extra money. You don't know what it's like working under someone in this line of work. Most girls go out on their own and make big money. I've always had trouble doing things on my own."

Here came the sob story, que the fucking violins. "Get up, walk to that last door down the hallway. Go inside and wait for me." I pointed down the long hall to my left. "Do you need me to hold your hand, or can you do one thing in your life by yourself?"

She turned her head to look down the hallway. She saw the menacing steel door at the end. I could smell the fear radiate from every orifice. "Did you hear me?" I snapped my fingers loud enough that she jumped in surprise.

"Is- is that your bedroom?" She asked shakily.

"Why would I send you to my bedroom? You think I would fuck you on my bed? You'll be lucky if I fuck you outside on the trashcans. Go to that room at the end of the hall, or get the fuck out of my house. I'll happily tell your boss what an irritating little bitch you've been."

She jumped up like a horse at the starting line of the Kentucky derby. "That's a good girl." I whispered to her as she walked hesitantly down that hall. I stopped so that she could walk the rest of the way on her own. She turned to look at me, her eyes begging for me to just fuck her on the couch and be done with it. "Keep that sweet little ass moving." I said, looking at my Rolex to see how much time had already been wasted, I only paid for the hour. Someone would come looking for her if she wasn't front and center with money in hand. I still had twenty-minutes of fun.

"Are you coming too?"

I looked up to see the girl standing just inches from the steel door. I gave her the first and only smile she would get tonight. "I'll be joining you in just a few seconds. I know I've been a bit harsh. I promise that's not really me. I'll go and grab you some extra money to take with you for your troubles." All the doubt and worry had left her completely. She smiled the most genuine smile any girl had ever given me.

"Don't play with your food!" I heard my late mothers voice in my head, reminding me of my manners.

"Sorry Mommy, I'll be a good boy." I said to myself as I opened the Living room coat closet. Jars of teeth lined the shelves behind my jackets. I reached towards the top, grabbing the jar containing my dentures that had been modified from bull shark teeth. The pearly white serrated edges, the chattering sound they made as I fished them from the jar, replacing them with my current set. I had to be very careful putting these babies in. Didn't want to cut my thumb again.

"Eat those long legs first. They look so juicy."

"I will mommy. I thought the exact same thing when I first laid eyes on this one." I closed the closet door, a gut wrenching scream came from the back room. She must have just turned on the light.

"What- what- what is this?"

The escort screamed as she came running back down the hall, only to fall into my grasp. I bit down on the first bit of exposed flesh I felt, my teeth sunk deep into her shoulder. Like all the others, she screamed bloody murder. I released so that I could experience the thrill of my catch. I wasn't expecting the bitch to jab her thumbnail into my fucking eye. "Goddamn! You bitch!" I shouted as I violently shoved her into the hallway wall. I grabbed my eye as the blood filled the palm of my hand. The antelope never fought back this way against the lion, it accepted it's fate the second it was caught in the lions powerful grasp. "You weren't supposed to do that. You don't know the rules. You aren't the fucking predator here!" I screamed in anger as I used my blood covered hand to punch a hole through the drywall. I reached down to grab the leg of my prey. Thunder rattled the walls and floor, the house went dark.

"Where are you, sweetie? I'm hungry!" I reached for her in the darkness but felt only the slick blood drenched hardwood floor. "You have nowhere to go. You can only hide for so long!"

A loud crash outside rattled the walls again. It sounded like the wind was ripping trees from the ground and tossing them. "You think anyone is going to come for you in this storm? You think the lights going out saved you? Well, you're wrong. The way I see it, you and I now have all the time in the world." The next loud crash sounded even closer to the outside of the house. Hopefully the windows hold.

"She is going to get away. You are going to end up right back in that place if you don't fix this mess!"

"I'm not going back to that place, mommy. I have this under control, I always have it under control." The lights flickered back on for only a second before cutting off again. "Did you like what you saw in that room? I hope it didn't frighten you too much. Fear sours the flesh, gives it this over powering metallic taste. So please, don't be afraid. The things you saw in my special room, they were never intended to scare anyone. It's all about how you interpret what you see."

I put my hand to the wall as I walked slowly. I knew there were limited hiding spots down this way. "Come out now, and I promise that we will make this quick and painless. There aren't too many hiding spots at this end of the house, so rest assured, I will find you." I knew it would be harder than I made it seem. This darkness was a hiding place all itself. "You didn't go back into that super scary room, did you?"

I felt my hand touch the red oak bathroom door. I reached down and twisted the handle gently. "Are you in here?" I asked as my mouth watered profusely. A flash of lightning lit up the room through the skylight above the tub. My reflection in the mirror scared the hell out of me. "Fuck!" I cried out at the sight of the blood covered, razor tooth, monster that stood before me.

"Afraid of your own reflection. Nothing ever changes."

"I'm not *'afraid'* of my reflection, mommy. It just startled me, that's all."

"Well, you better find that little whore before she gets away. I refuse to sit in that place with you when they lock you back up."

"We're not going back there, mommy. I promise. I will get the whore and eat her right up." There was another loud crash, only this time it came from inside the house, right in the next room. "I can taste you now. Just come the fuck out. I'm hungry!"

Stupidly, I ran full speed in the pitch black. My face smacked the corner of the door. I went flying back, hitting my head on the toilet bowl.

"You idiot! Don't start making silly mistakes now!"

"I'm sorry, mommy. It won't happen again."

I stood up as my head spun in the darkness. I reached up to feel a large gash right under my hairline. I felt my way through the bathroom slowly. Mommy was right, I'm an idiot. Suddenly, the power came back on. The lights in the hallway lit up, showing the puddle of blood that covered the floor. I waited for a moment for them to cut back off, but they didn't.

"How fucking scared are you now, baby?!" I growled as I barged into the bedroom next door. I flipped on the light switch, scanning the room for any signs that the whore had been here. The room was spotless, not a single thing had been touched or moved. "Fucking whore!" I growled even louder. Without a second thought, I kicked in the door across the hall. It flung open, smacking the wall hard enough that it knocked a picture frame to the floor. I flipped the switch. My workout room was also undefiled, not a single weight out of place. I started getting increasingly angry. That was, until I remembered there was only one room left for the whore to be in. I turned off the lights to my gym and focused my attention to the last door in the hallway. "I gave you a chance for this to end painlessly. You have officially pissed away a chance at mercy."

"Come and get me, you deranged fuckhead!"

I smiled at the invitation. "With pleasure, bitch." I opened the thick steel door. The room was still dark. "You are a brave little girl, sitting in this room all alone in the dark. I'm sure you've noticed that this room has a closet door that's locked from the inside. Well, I'll let you in on a little secret, it's not a closet." I flipped the light switch, bracing myself for the crazed whore to charge at me. The light flickered on. I smiled at the beauty that I had worked so long and hard creating. "This is years of hard work. I hope you have taken the time to appreciate the things you've seen. Not many have seen them and lived to bask in its glory." I looked around the room, sniffing the air. "I know you're in here sweet-"

Before I could finish, something hard smashed into the back of my head. I fell forward into the pile of human bones that carpeted the floor. Skulls, femurs, ribs, a few spines, went flying in all directions when I hit the floor with a thunderous pop. Before I was able to regain my composure, I was struck again with a hard object. This time, in the back of the neck.

"How does that feel, mother fucker?!" The whore screamed as she hit me again and again.

Eventually, my body had grown numb from the vicious blows. The room started spinning. I could see the pieces of myself hanging on the walls, all the work I put into taking them off. A few more hard strikes and I was seeing spots. One more, and it was lights out. I came to as I sat in the dog kennel under mommy's front porch. "Mommy, I'm hungry. Can I please eat now?" I heard mommy's rocking chair stop on the old porch above my head. Mommy got up and walked to the railing. I could see her looking down at me, her eyes burning with hatred.

"Has it grown yet? Has your pee-pee come in? I bet your still just a nasty little girl who will grow up to be some filthy whore. You won't come out until I have the big, strong, son that I wanted."

My stomach growled. I had lost count of how many days it had been since I had eaten. "I would make one grow if I could, mommy. I promise I would. Please, let me out!"

My mother stared at me for a moment before smiling big enough that I could see those rotted black teeth.

"If I let you out, you put on the skin. You got it?"

My stomach knotted up. Not just from hunger, but from fear. "I'll wear the skin, mommy. Can I please just eat?" I heard my mother's footsteps as she walked over to the back door. I knew she was going to get the skin. I looked down at my filthy, nude body. I wished so bad to be the boy mommy wanted. Why did I have to be what I was? I heard the back door open, and my mother's footsteps once again walking across the rickety porch. She dropped the skin over the railing. It flopped like a Thanksgiving ham hitting the kitchen floor. I didn't want to put that thing on. The sight of it made me want to puke. The lock on my cage popped open as my mother stood in front of my kennel.

"Put that on, sweet boy. I'll make you a real nice dinner."

My mother smiled as she walked away. I looked down at the skin. The thought of food helped me stomach through putting it on. I walked in the house, the skin getting tighter the more I moved in it.

My mother stood by the stove. She stirred the giant pot in front of her. The smell of baked beans and cornbread filled the small kitchen. My stomach moaned like an angry bull.

"You go and get some pants on to cover up that wee-wee of yours, son. I'm certainly proud of it, just don't need it flapping around the house."

Little drops of spit flew into the giant steaming pot as my mother laughed. The skin was already making me so hot that sweat started dripping from the tip of my nose. "Mommy, this thing is hot. Isn't there something else I could wear instead? I'm sweating so bad." I moaned even as my mother removed the giant wooden spoon from the pot and pointed it just inches from my face.

"You'll wear it until you grow out of it. After that, we will get you a bigger one. The bottom isn't the only part we have to worry about. Soon you'll have boobies, and every man in town will want to pass you around. We will have to tape them down for now. We'll get a top to the skin later."

My mother's hatred for me was always so much more bearable when I wore the skin. She treated me like the child she always wanted.

"Wake the fuck up, freak!"

I jolted awake from the ice-cold water being poured over my head. "Son of a bitch!" I cried out in pain.

Once my eyes adjusted to the room, I could see the escort standing in front of me, holding a bucket she found in the garage. I tried to reach for her, but my hands were zipitied to the kitchen chair that I had been placed in while unconscious. "What- what the fuck is this shit? You going to call the cops, tell them all about me?" I spit the water that had dripped from my lips right in her face. She stared at me, completely unfazed.

"I've looked all around this place while you were crying for your mommy in your sleep. I'll say this about you, you are one sick and twisted fuck."

I noticed the bandaging around her shoulder. Must have found that pesky first aid kit under the kitchen sink. "Yeah, so what?" I asked, just noticing that my shark teeth were no longer in my mouth. I looked up at the whore as she frowned at me. Her disapproving looks meant that she had a lot more on her mind.

"You're right. I am going to call the cops and report your sorry fucking ass. But before I do that-"

She stopped mid-sentence. Her face told me one thing. My make-up had come off due to the water thrown at me. I could tell she had so many questions. "Before you ask, yes, I am a woman. The stuff that you saw in that back bedroom were things that were taken off, and out of me during various surgeries." I couldn't even begin to read her expression at this point. It looked as if she had just grabbed ahold of an electric fence. "Yes, I kill other women. Whores, mostly. I've been doing it for years. I take a fuck ton of testosterone and work out at the highest level. I take being a man very seriously. I even-"

She put her hand in my face like I had done to her earlier. *"How have you gotten away with this for so long? How have you not been caught? Someone must come looking for the girls you've killed. Someone cares about them."*

I couldn't help but smile at her. It was so cute how fucking stupid she was. "No one comes and looks for whores. You and the rest of them are worth nothing. Some of you have pimps that come asking, but with the right amount of money, they forget all about you. And I haven't been caught because I am good at what I do, I don't make mistakes." She smiled at me. I knew she was going to call me out, she thought she was so clever.

"Looks like you made the mistake of underestimating me. You thought I was going to be some helpless victim. Well, you were wrong. I'm not the one who is helpless and weak, you are."

I would have given her a standing ovation, if it were possible at this moment in time. "You are still the victim. You are still helpless and at my mercy, you just don't realize it yet."

Before I could blink, I was slapped upside the head with the giant bucket that was used in awaking me. It whacked my head so hard, I almost passed out again. Thunder rumbled outside. The wind started picking up again. "Do you really think the police are going to come rescue some whore in the middle of a goddamn hurricane? They wouldn't come to the rescue of a beaten prostitute on a normal day. What in the fuck makes you think they'll come now?" I could tell that comment stung, just a little.

"So, spitting water in your face doesn't phase you, but telling you how insignificant you are *does?*" I laughed as the whore turned her head, only to hide her shame. "Let's just get one thing straight, this night will not have a happy ending for you. You will never see the sunrise, your life will end very soon. This isn't some cheesy horror film where the girl plunges a knife into the villain's neck and escapes by jumping from the closest window. The sooner you can accept that, the better off the rest of your short life will be."

She sat down on the edge of the coffee table in front of me. I could still see hope behind those blue eyes. Hope was a fickle mistress; hope was the motto of the desperate.

"What makes you so sure that it will be 'me' that dies here tonight? You are the one zip-tied to a chair. I could grab a knife from the kitchen right now and slit your throat. After the police find all the fucked-up shit lying around this house, they won't be looking for who killed the fucking psychopath tied to a chair."

The more she spoke, the more hope I could see filling her mind with frivolous non-sense. Maybe I should put her in the pool out back. It hasn't been cleaned in over two years, and the rain must have added enough water to overfill it. "If you're going to kill me, at least take the money from my safe. I'd rather you have it than the greedy government."

She looked around curiously. She was like a stupid fish about to bite a big shiny hook. "It's not out here, silly. Its in the room behind the locked door. If you knock, it will open." Her eyes darted towards the silver door at the end of the hall. I could tell she was reluctant to go back in my special room, but she wanted the money so badly it was like watching a heavy smoker go an hour without a drag.

"The door will just open if I knock? I've never seen a door do that without someone opening it from the inside. How do I know this isn't a trick?"

I didn't know if I should complement her wherewithal to circumspect my sudden act of kindness, or call her a ditzy bitch. "The door is set on sound activation. You've never seen such a thing because it was something I created myself. Besides, you've never been even close to someone with my amount of wealth and knowledge."

I could see the gears in her tiny brain try to turn, thinking didn't seem to be one of her strengths. "What is the worst that could happen? I am still strapped to this chair with nowhere to go. Why not go and take a quick peak?" She stood up slowly, still staring down at the door. "Is it the bones scattered amongst the floor that frightens you, or what's hanging on the walls?"

I pictured the skin I had used as wallpaper, the pieces taken from me put up on a crude but beautiful shrine. My very own house of pain.

"Your creepy decorations don't frighten me anymore. The fact that you are a lying, manipulative, piece of shit does."

"I guess you can just kill me and leave without checking. Makes no difference to me if you leave here a wealthy whore or not." She looked around the room for a moment before grabbing an antique candlestick holder from the end-table beside the couch.

"Looks like you are ready to take on the world." I said with a snake like hiss.

Knock Knock

Both of us locked eyes on my front door. I knew it had to be the fucking police or her pimp, either would be rather inconvenient now. "You may have just gotten really lucky." I said growling through my teeth. The escort walked behind me, to my utter surprise she started pushing my chair around the corner, just far enough that my unexpected visitor wouldn't see from the doorway.

"I'm impressed." I giggled, looking up at her.

"Just shut the fuck up and don't make a sound." She whispered harshly in my ear before giving herself a once over in

the mirror. I heard her pop open the dead bolt and unlatch the chain. She opened the door to greet whoever it was.

"Hello Miss, my name is Peter Becket. I live a few houses down. I was just wanting to run over now that the storm has calmed down and check to see if everyone was alright. That darn wind really did a number on the neighborhood.

I rolled my eyes hearing Peter's voice. He was an annoying little turd, always saying hi and trying to make small talk every fucking time I walked out the door.

"Are you a friend of Marcus? He has so many young ladies coming over its hard to keep track. What happened to your poor shoulder? You should get that bandaged up."

Peter did that forced laugh that people do when they don't want to come off like a nosey prick. I bet he was wearing that stupid safety vest that he wore when he went on his little nightly jogs with his fat bitch wife. "I tripped in the basement when the power went out. I was just about to clean it up when you knocked. And Marcus is actually in the shower right now, I'll let him know that you stopped by to check on him." The conversation hit an awkward silence, and I knew exactly why.

"You tripped in the basement? Well, you must've landed on your head as well. No houses in this neighborhood have basements. Heck, most houses in California don't have basements. It's because of earthquakes and whatnot."

I couldn't believe this dumb bitch. Why didn't she just say she fell in the garage? Walked into a mirror? Any fucking thing. "Silly me. I meant the garage. I'm not from around here, so I get a little confused at times." There was another awkward silence before the escort said goodnight and slammed the door shut.

"Wow, you should have pursued acting instead of sucking dick. You were a natural." I said sarcastically as the escort pulled my chair back to where it was before we were interrupted. She didn't say a word as she picked back up the candlestick holder.

"You know, you really should have told Peter what was going on here, but you get to decide your own fate. I'm still tied up, not much I can do." She chose once again not to respond. "Have you ever watched that movie called Peeping Tom? If not, I recommend it."

She walked into the kitchen, still ignoring me. I heard her rummage through some of the drawers. I knew she was looking for a more practical weapon to defend herself against the possible horrors that awaited her. She returned with a large butchers knife that I kept in the woodblock on the counter. I could see my reflection in the stainless steel blade.

"I'm going to see if you are full of shit or not. Regardless, I'm slitting your throat when I get back."

Before I could give my rebuttal, the escort was already halfway down the hall. The light glared off the large blade she held at the ready. The second she was through the steel door, I yanked up with my left arm, snapping the zip tie like tissue paper. I crept slowly down the hall and towards the steel door that now sat wide open. I could hear the escort yanking on the other door handle. I guess she forgot to knock. I looked down, making sure my shadow didn't cast into the room where she could turn and see. The door rattled a few more times before finally, there was a loud knock. My heart raced with excitement. I peeked around the corner. There she was, back to me, knocking heavily on the dark wooden door in front of her. The lock from the inside clicked, and the door creaked open.

"Who the fuck are you?"

The escort screamed as she stepped on a femur bone. It rolled under her foot, sending her flat on her ass. My mother crawled slowly from the darkness, my lack of feeding her started to make her resemble a living skeleton. Only a few patches of her thin white hair remained.

"Get the fuck away from me lady!"

The escort screamed as she scooted away as quickly as she could. The butchers knife made a loud *'whooshing'* sound as the whore swung it around in front of her. Mother's puke and shit covered gown drug across the dirty floor, her uncut nails dug deep into the wood as she dragged herself closer and closer. She looked like a real-life monster. I smiled at the glorious sight. If only mommy could see herself now, not that she could anymore, she went blind a year or so ago.

"I said stay the fuck back, you crazy bitch!"

The large knife sliced through the air again and again. "Get her mommy. Get her!" I cheered to the surprise of the escort who hadn't noticed me behind her until now. My excitement must have distracted my mother. She raised her head up towards the sound of my voice. She needed me now, she depended on me. It was time to take her out of this room and make things a-

"Bitch!"

I looked in my mothers face just as the knife sliced right across her throat. The cut opened instantly; dark red blood sprayed out like a busted water pipe. "No!" I screamed as I jumped down to the floor to try and stop the bleeding. Gallons of my mother's blood covered my chest and lap. Her body started to convulse, she wrapped her wrinkled hands around my wrist. The last thing my mother heard was my pleas that she hold on a little longer. "Fuck! Fuck!" I screamed as I pulled her lifeless body up to my chest. "I'm sorry mommy. I'm sorry I kept you in that room for so long. I just wanted you to depend on me. I needed you to want me!" I cried harder than I ever had.

"You are a fucking freak. You sick, twisted mother fucker."

I looked up at the whore. She leaned forward, jabbing the knife into my stomach. The pain was indescribable. All the breath exited my lungs with such velocity that it felt like my chest had exploded. "You- fucking- bitch." I choked on the shit that came pouring from my mouth, the metallic taste of my own blood. The escort pulled the knife from my gut. More and more blood spewed out onto my mothers corpse, and all the bones that surrounded it. The escort got to her feet. The knife in her hand dripped a cruel mixture of my mother and I. With both hands, she stepped forward, jabbing the blade deep into my chest. There was a loud crunch before I fell to my side.

"Fuck your money! Fuck your mommy! And fuck you!"

The whore used her bare foot to kick the black handle of the knife, sending it deep enough to pierce through the back of my once white dress-shirt. In my fading moments, I could hear her whisper something in my ear.

"Not so fucking stupid after all, you piece of shit."

I opened my eye's just long enough to see her walking out the steel door and into the hallway. She had the twenty-five-hundred dollars from my pocket in hand. She turned to look at me one last time. *"If somehow you survive long enough to get hungry, you always have mommy."*

She laughed maniacally, before shutting off the light and slamming the steel door shut.

"Where the fuck have you been, Kim? That was a lot longer than a fucking hour. Rich dude better have paid you extra. What the hell happened to your shoulder? He get rough?"

Kim handed the skinny pimp known as "Shifty" the wad of money without saying a word. She watched as he counted it. She knew if she was lucky, she would get two hundred from it. Kim was relieved when she was handed four one-hundred-dollar bills. "What's all this for?" Kim asked trying to not sound ungrateful for the shady pimp's sudden growth of a heart. He looked up at her and shrugged as he played with his '*hard earned*' loot.

"Looks like you've had a tough night. Figured whatever shit went down, you earned that extra. Lot of girls have been going missing in this area. Keep your eyes open and your mouth shut."

Shifty stuffed the money into his front pocket. He turned and entered the back door of the strip club, the purple and pink lights flickered with the beat of the overly loud rock music that blared over the speakers. Kim looked down at the money. She knew Shifty was a white trash, piece of wannabe gangster shit, but she appreciated being treated fairly for once. Kim thought about Marcus, the horrible things she had seen and been through. The money that must be hidden away somewhere in that house of hell. Kim thought about returning to the house, but decided against it. As soon as the television and radio stations got wind of the events, the story spread like a wildfire.

"The House of horrors" An upscale home in the Bateman area of California where the estimated remains of forty-two women were found in various stages of decomposition. Police say that a concerned neighbor named Peter Becket called to have a wellness check on his neighbor and friend after not seeing him for a few days. Investigators say that the bodies of Marcus Cash and Martha Glennbury were found locked inside a room at the end of the property. Cash and Glennbury both suffered fatal wounds from a large kitchen knife. We are being told that Cash is the homeowner and perpetrator of these heinous crimes. Detective Bravora of the LAPD homicide division has stated Mrs. Glennbury

was discovered to be missing from her room at the Hillview assisted living center. Mrs. Glennbury suffered from severe Alzheimer's. It was believed she had just wandered off. We now know that wasn't the case. Mrs. Glennbury's family said they were shocked and saddened that anyone would do such a thing to such a loving, caring soul.

Though the events in Bateman County continued to haunt Kim, she moved on with her life. She moved to Arkansas to live with her Aunt Kathy. From there, she would go back to school and earn a degree in business management. Kim's life changed drastically when she was granted full custody of her son Thomas on February 8th, 1982. Kim now lives in Iowa, where she and her new husband run a successful pet grooming business. Kim still thinks about Marcus, and the tragic day she knocked on his door in Bateman County California. As crazy as it sounds, sometimes she feels like he's still out there somewhere.

"Healing doesn't mean the damage never existed. It means the damage no longer controls our lives."

Author- Unknown

ABOUT THE AUTHOR

Stuart Bray lives with his wife and two sons in Salem, Ky. He is a life-long horror fan, his favorites include The Texas chainsaw massacre (1974) Halloween (1978) Maniac (1980) in his free time Stuart is the host of the murder shed podcast. A show discussing lesser-known serial killers and horror movie reviews. You can follow Stuart Bray on Instagram, Twitter, Slasher App, Hive, and Tumblr.

@Stuart_bray_1991

Made in the USA
Columbia, SC
02 November 2023

25366393R00086